T0345531

Efina

THE SWISS LIST

A YOUNG WOMAN GOES TO THE THEATRE one Thursday. She sees two men on stage, two actors who enter alternately. One with a paunch, a swindler. The other, lean and calm, a man of some eminence. When the play is over, one actor takes his bows, and upon seeing him she understands: he had been two men at once. He's standing at the edge of the stage, the young woman is in the third row. She can see the powder masking the pores of his skin and count every hair on his head. She can tell herself that his smiles are for her, his eyes are not gazing into the reflectors, they are seeking hers at the same time. So who can this wonderful actor be. The name explodes from all sides of the theatre: this actor's name is T. Right, this man's name is T. His face means nothing to her. His body is unrecognizable. But the name is a memory. In the young woman's life, this name has already existed. There was a letter. A letter was written, she doesn't know

1

when, nor for what reason it was sent. This man, young and dark-haired a few years ago, today paunchy and grey. A young, sturdy man. A page of his writing, he had held it in his hands and his mind had rested on it for several minutes. The young woman goes through the cardboard boxes lying all over her junk room—that letter, did she keep it, did she throw it into the wastebasket. There were changes of residence, there were departures, there were men. Did the letter go from house to house in a box. Was it in the attic when she changed houses and men. Was it asleep in its envelope during break-up scenes. Was it disintegrating into particles while supper was cooking, when the telephone remained silent or when, from her bed or couch, her mind nowhere wandered.

The actor is in the foyer of the theatre. She fails to recognize his features, but it is T all right, or at least people say so and his name is on the programme. The crowd is pushing her towards the door, she has to walk past him. T sees her and says hello and yes, now she can congratulate him. She leaves him thinking of the letter. She doesn't remember if she answered it, and back in her flat, she writes down words she knows he will not read.

Efina

T, she writes, she cannot write dear, as he is not dear to her, that's what she doesn't understand and that's why she's writing. T, she writes, I saw you tonight on stage and as I said when I was coming out, I was carried away by your acting. I don't know if the play is good. The production was not bad and the set seemed fine to me. But the subtlety of your acting carried me far away from here. I went to places I could hardly remember. I saw hours and hours of films on TV again. I visited all kinds of prisons in America, I saw the faces of men I had only spied on in lifts. I could see on your skin what you meant to express. I perceived it without missing a thing and you propelled me out of space and time. You became all men. Thanks to you, for a whole hour, I forgot that my name is Efina, that soon I'll be thirty-two, I forgot I live in this city in a three-room flat with eastern exposure, along with two spindly spiders. My neighbours are deaf and listen to TV from night till morning. I take out the rubbish on Tuesdays. I have dinner with friends. My curtains are never drawn. Here is what I had to tell you: it is possible that in the past I did not get your letter as you probably wished. I no longer know what I thought and I don't know what happened. Tell me—the question is trotting through my head—did you ever get an answer from me. I remember my surprise when I read you, I opened the envelope, the letter became dazzling and I could not understand it. Here I am going to end and there is only one more thing to tell you: I would not like you to think my letter is one of those love letters, or to see it that way. There is no love between us. Something different, perhaps, that we are free to express or to silence. I would rather say it right away: as for me, I do not wish that thing to return. It is possible that we may come across each other by chance. I hope you will no longer receive my compliments with eyes fixed on the floor. That smile sets off ideas in me I cannot define but that drive me mad. When I left you, I had to lean against the wall and a taxi driver asked if I needed his help. A man tried to sell me drugs. Another asked me how much I charge. My neighbours watched me as I walked up the stairs, they noticed the state I was in and they thought that in a while something serious or difficult would happen.

After ending her letter in this way, she closes it carefully. She makes sure the edges are firmly glued down with saliva. The address is unknown to her, she could just open the phone book and find it. She puts the envelope on her desk where it waits for seventeen months. Then she moves, and throws it away.

AFTER THE EVENING AT THE THEATRE, T tells the woman he lives with the story of this meeting: the young woman he saw again, who had not answered. Or who had answered, in his mind things get confused and he retains nothing. If an answer did come one day, it went up in smoke in the fire of the dump a long time ago. The woman he lives with is not listening. The letter was written at a time when she had nothing to do with T. For the next few days, T thinks of writing. He does not know that woman, she is neither interesting nor especially likeable. He writes a letter anyway.

Madame, he wants to write, but the woman is still young, perhaps younger than he is; he writes her first name, the tone is too casual, he doesn't know how to begin, he settles on Dear Efina, although he thinks she is not dear to him and it bores him to write. There only one thing to straighten out and everything will be over.

Dear Efina, he scrawls, I am writing to you because it seems to me that one thing remains to be settled, something that had been hanging in the air for years and we thought had been laid to rest. We both felt it at the theatre the other night. You can't say no, I felt it in your voice, in your way of throwing words out any old way. I must have kept my eyes down for I could not let you see the jumble within me. I was afraid you would realize it and at any rate this is not something women like you should see. Women like you are fragile. Women like you fall to pieces. Women of your kind are prone and quick to fall in love and you know I have someone. I have three sons and a daughter somewhere else and no intention whatsoever of starting over again. And at any rate you know very well that love is not what drives me. You know as well as I do that love is not the only way for men and women to come together—the range of what links us together is vast and subtle. Let us not allow novels and films to simplify us. Now I return to the time of that letter. Yes, I must indeed have written a letter. Years ago, I thought only of writing to you. I remember the exact spot. I recall the light of the place and the colour of the cheap plywood desk where I was sitting. It was a bright day, and yet it was autumn. I know exactly what steps, what strides I made and the walk that made me suddenly decide to sit down in front of the paper. A certain pond surely has something to do with certain silly turns of phrase I may have, in certain places, formulated. The birds and the leaves of the trees are no doubt also responsible for a bit of twaddle that may have floated into my letter. But I do not want to return to what was at the bottom of all this. What the words may have expressed and what I may have asked I do not wish to find out. There is nothing more to think about. All I want from you is to see, as you showed in the theatre, your skin, young but wrinkled, your eyes panicked in their deep-set shadows, under your make-up, which, by the way, you apply rather poorly. Your cheeks may still fool people, your hair is badly done and you have ten or fifteen years left to claim you can still be a lover.

T raises his head for a moment. He wonders if he'll go on or if here he should stop. He thinks of tearing it all up. He doesn't do this, and the sheet of paper on the kitchen table lingers there for ever. His girlfriend goes through it at breakfast. Every day she reads sentences aloud to him. She calls the letter the soap opera and T, with her, laughs at that.

EFINA HAS MOVED TO ANOTHER PART of the city. If T comes to mind, she drives him away. He's nothing to her, no. Life turns its crank and in Efina's belly a little frog is growing. Arms surround her on the pillow. The sun floods her bedroom, her bedroom faces south. Efina goes to work. No there is no room for T. The only room for T is on the programmes of plays. His name pops up like a mushroom in the list of actors three or four times a year. Efina takes time to peruse the programmes, to find out the places where T is playing, and which evenings. In her letterbox sometimes, T's silhouette lands on fliers advertising the theatre. The photos are artistic, you can hardly see anything, but Efina would recognize him even if she only saw his back. Even his foot. Even his toe she thinks she would recognize, but of course that's not true and other women in this city know his toes admirably. Sometimes she sees the names of pretty actresses in these lists. She scornfully imagines what's going on in the dressing rooms. Entanglements develop rather frequently in dressing rooms. Dressing rooms provide test tubes for all sorts of fermentations. A certain play showed one of these actresses in her panties on the last page of the newspaper. She was lying in T's arms. The article said that the play had some daring scenes in it. Strong, hot scenes. Not to be shown to children. Scenes where T was naked. The actress naked too, it seemed. Let him play whatever they want him to play, it's all the same to her and it only annoys Efina because, she doesn't know why.

T DURING THIS TIME WROTE other letters. They are hidden in the wardrobe. He has in a box shoes he never wears because they hurt his feet. The letters are under the shoes. Today T is at the beginning of a period of unemployment. He gets the box and from under the shoes takes out a letter.

Dear Efina, it reads, I must take another piece of paper and write these words again. I thought everything had been said but I realize that other pages arise behind that letter I wrote I don't know how many years, generations, ago to you. Solid pages which are not going to dissolve by themselves. Pages that weigh and pull. Pages that make screens. I can't help thinking of those pages as monoliths that cannot be overcome simply with a sculptor's tool. They have to be cut with a saw. You would have to set up a work site and a lot more strength would be needed than you can possibly imagine. I do not know where you live and I won't try to find out, for you are of no importance in my life. My life is full to the brim. My life overflows from all sides. I have four children to support, plus a demanding companion, other women I must satisfy and whom I have completely forgotten, quite apart from my bank account that must every month be satisfied, too. I would not find the smallest interstice in my life for you to fill, Efina, even though I know that you are supple, your waist is flexible and slim and your arms could fold sixteen times if someone wanted to do that. I write this even though I am of course not sure, I say what I imagine, thinking of your puny name. How strange that I'm not talking and must still write to you. This method is slow, out of date. Paper must be destroyed. Letters must be stored, but in fact why keep them—one has no time to reread them. I return constantly to that first letter.

One day, I was in front of a desk and my thoughts sorted themselves out under your eyes. What made me write to you, what was so pressing, so important. I was asking you for a favour. I begged you and you rejected me anyway. The mud with which we were moulded must have sealed your eyelids. But now, you see me. Yes, I do change appearances, but that's my job, you know that. My eyes are black and shining. I can change them at will, I have round, small, narrow eyes. I have also had blue eyes. I can appear stocky or thin at will, but when I come back to my body, it is corpulent and robust. I tend to be plump, a tendency I fight by circling the park. I have thick, short hair. I shave my cheeks every morning. I do not wear glasses. I do not smoke, I drink very little. I walk silently. My shoe size is 8½. My mouth can take on any shape, my lips are chameleons. They say my person exudes a certain magnetism. I'm writing all this so you may remember I exist, and just about the same as in the past.

T turns the page and chooses another passage: I'm speaking today of course about things that are obsolete. For, I insist on saying it again, you are today as close to me as the women I pass by on the street and if the name Efina was called out, fifty of them would turn their heads.

Months have gone by and Efina's womb gives birth to a baby. Efina is very busy. No she does not think of T. She does not think of T when she nurses the baby. She does not think of T when she wheels the stroller. She does not think of T. She thinks only of the baby. She bathes, she changes her baby. She mashes carrots for the baby. She thinks only of the baby and what babies coming from T might look like. She wonders if with T her womb could have conceived a still prettier baby, with still more dimples, a baby sweet as honey, who does not cry every night and never stops peeing. Efina imagines that coming from T, babies are sweets that turn into little boys. Into rowdy adolescents. Into stocky men like T. Why did T grow bald. Is he really bald or does he shave his head for the theatre. Does he really have a big belly or did he eat cookies to comply with the wishes of directors in order to fit different roles.

Efina

Efina buys a dog the colour of candied chestnuts. She takes him for walks in the forest. The dog at first is high-spirited, then he changes personality. It must be because he's growing. He is a pleasure to look at. Light shimmers on his back. He has an elegant way of walking, he sinks his four paws into an elastic mass. The dog goes into a thicket and comes out immediately. His coat is clean and shiny. He trots smoothly along ahead of her. His head turns and his muzzle lifts up to look at her.

Efina moves to the other end of the city. She eats alone at home. She has no need for a man growing heavy at her side. She admits she has no need for that, she would rather go forward alone. The baby counts for peanuts. She goes to the theatre and before making a reservation, she looks through the cast to see if T is performing, and if he is, she gives up the idea of seeing the play. That's too bad, for T performs a great deal, so she deprives herself of many plays. He has reached the age in which directors find him perfect for his looks and style of acting. She's sometimes afraid of running into him on the street. That can happen, the city is big but occasionally one does bump into friends. But even if she passed by T, she would probably be unable to recognize him. She looks at men on the bus. Men look at her too and feel obliged to ask if they know each other.

SOME TIME LATER, SOME OF EFINA'S girlfriends invite her to the theatre. She doesn't look at the programme but it's as if she knew it, because in the car she babbles away as if she were a girl on the day of her first communion. For T makes his entrance. He's slim and has a good head of hair, or could T be wearing a wig and is he wearing a corset compressing his belly. Efina does not listen. She concentrates on the air T is filtering into her organism. She concentrates on the way his lips come together, on the rise of his Adam's apple, on his pudgy, mobile fingers. She wonders if he has hair on his body and at what time he shaves. If he has an electric razor. The colour of his bathroom. The play is over, her friends are having a drink at the bar. One by one, the actors come out of the dressing rooms like rats. Efina could leave. She could take the bus. She could say that her head, her migraines, her stomach. But she has the urge to see T. She tells herself that after so many years, years and years, she could see T just once. He does not even remember her and she doesn't care about him. After all these years and years and years.

T is sitting in their circle. Efina's girlfriends are wild about T and they joke with him. They say his full name. Efina adopts the attitude of a calm, reserved woman. She says hello to T and glancing at her, he says hello too. He has grown softer and older, his neck is withered and wrinkled. On his brow one can see his worries. His head is leaning forward, he should take better care of his appearance. A roll of fat bulges over his belt. Efina calculates that with a little care he could look young and slim, yes if he exercised more. Does T in his free time think of working out. T in a tracksuit, in shorts. T pedalling away in a gym. Or in a bathing suit at the pool. T, a silly-looking man. A man with bags under his eyes, with thinning hair through which his skull is showing and hairs in his ears. A worn-out man, slightly pitiful in his way of innocently offering his face as if he were attractive. His eyes are sharp, tiny. His eyes have become light, whereas what used to make T's face were two dark cavities. T is over the hill, he left his charm on the stage. The lights are going down. His image is grey,

it is fading. From T's mouth flat syllables are issu-
ing. The nape of his neck is soft and curved. He
doesn't smoke any more. He orders a glass of min-
eral water. The friends laugh and exclaim: T . . . !
Efina goes to the toilet. When she comes back, T is
talking with other people at the bar. In the car her
friends are going into raptures again: T the seducer,
the charmer, the handsome actor women love. Efina
definitively writes him off.

T IN HIS BED THINKS BACK over the evening at the
theatre. His acting was very good, his acting is getting more and more subtle. Too bad the other actors
were not up to his level. Other actors sometimes spoil
the pleasure of acting. And those women at the bar.
They were a bit overexcited. And that Efina in the
midst of them. Efina was with them, he can hardly
believe it, he can't possibly associate her with that
group of female admirers. Perhaps because she didn't
speak. Perhaps because she hardly smiled. Perhaps
because she had no shape. Or because it was clear that
she was lost in her thoughts. That Efina is an unpleasant woman, after all, T feels uncomfortable round
her. When he's round her, he counts his words and

his whole self becomes mechanical. He's not quite himself in the presence of that Efina. Luckily he did not send her the letters he's been writing to her for ages. Luckily, and that business is finally settled: the woman means nothing to T any more. Besides, the proof is, he felt no emotion. He wasn't even surprised, in no way did he feel transported or even stirred. T tells himself that his only feeling when he saw Efina in the red armchair, with her glass in her hand, was to wonder if it was champagne she was drinking. Or was it white wine. Yes, probably a sparkling wine, they have those in the theatre. Prosecco, no doubt. T had the idea of having a glass of champagne. But he ordered water and those women assaulted him. No, really not even one little spark of emotion upon discovering Efina sitting in the foyer of the theatre. His heart did not pound wildly. T did not turn red. He greeted her calmly. He noticed her jewellery. Were her jewellery gold or were they junk earrings. Junk, Efina is not refined. She is not a woman of taste. T likes women of taste. The conversation developed and at no point did T feel like talking to her. At absolutely no time in the course of the evening. Besides, he'd have nothing to say to her. So . . . that business is over. Yes it is completely over, since T even noticed the shoes Efina wears. And that he found really regrettable. Feet have some importance for T. He likes women in high heels. He understands it isn't practical and may even give them a backache. But T thinks a woman can't move about unless she's at least two or three inches higher. Two or three inches lower, T is of the opinion that a woman is not a woman. Under two inches, a woman is a human being. T did not at all appreciate the things Efina wears on her feet. A glance was enough for him: Efina is uninteresting. It's because she is uninteresting that he was able to spend the evening almost twenty inches away from her without his body getting all worked up. He did not notice the slightest emotion. He did not think about her skin. He did not think about her legs. On the contrary, he felt irritated by the movements of her eyes. Can't she look straight ahead, T kept saying to himself all evening while Efina was staring at her glass or at the table. So that T wonders if her eyes are brown, or black. And why does she insist on wearing that eyeshadow. That blue is not the right colour for her. That blue would be right for a blonde, not for a regular brunette like her. Could she possibly think she's a blonde. Could she possibly think she's striking. Could that Efina think she can get away with wearing make-up as if she were beautiful. She isn't, and how insane of him to have written those letters to her. Those letters were pure fantasy, he wrote to a woman who does not exist. He must write to the real one and the other will be erased.

That night he gets up and sits at the table. He takes out his lined writing pad. Efina, he writes, and this time the idea does not come to write Dear, Dear Friend, or My Dear, as he dared to write a few times. I saw you this evening at the theatre . . . No, that's not right. He begins again, another sheet of paper. Efina, we saw each other at the theatre. Forgive me if I am writing in this blunt, frank way. I feel the need to tell you that you are not close to me. I thought I sensed under your eyelids a few interested glances. Let me say it once and for all: you are nothing. Nothing ever happened. It is silly of you to think that we might be having a relationship. I have a woman in my life, and—forgive me if I am hurting you—she is infinitely more precious to me than all the women I know. Including you, Efina. You must get that through your head. Since we are, somehow, strangely, old acquaintances, allow me to tell you this: pay attention to your manners and be more careful about what you wear. If you wish men to find you attractive, never look as if you're afraid your presence is boring them. Drink champagne or red wine. Stop using eye shadow. Try to look happier and more friendly. Men want to have fun. Talk a little, move, laugh. You look like a mute. Excuse me for saying this to you, I somehow feel for you a kind of lingering tenderness, still, and I feel somewhat responsible for seeing you in this state. At that moment, T's companion wakes up and she calls for him to come to bed. T leaves the letter and joins his girlfriend who no longer feels like sleeping. The next day he disposes of the letter. But Efina does not leave him. He realizes that he must write to her. Yes, write to her once and for all, and it will all be blotted out. Write to the woman he saw.

Efina, he writes, I'm taking the liberty of writing to you since we ran into each other the other night. We were unable to speak to each other and I feel the necessity of filling up yet another page. As soon as I saw you, I realized that nothing had happened between us. This is what I wanted to tell you: it was all nothing, it's all dead and I feel relieved. I'm sure you feel the same way. But perhaps you already knew we had nothing to say to each other and you are perhaps wondering why I took up my pen again. It's because I want everything to be clear. I want to cut off all connections. You are extremely indifferent to me, you are just an ordinary person and I hope that's what I am for you. I want you to find happiness in this life for, if I may say so, you did not exactly seem radiant to me. My best to you, T.

He's furious with his letter. The words are still too connected, too attached to that woman. She's going to think he wants to see her again, whereas he's saying exactly the opposite. He picks up a blank sheet of paper: Madame, You will no doubt be surprised to get a letter from me for the second time in your life. I have but one thing to tell you: I am so deeply sorry to have written the first one. When I saw you the other evening, I realized I had made a mistake and you couldn't possibly have given me what I was asking for. You have no idea how relieved I am. You are not at all my type and you were quite right not to have answered—we are not people of the same sort. Yours very sincerely.

The letter is still too furious. T tries a fourth version. Madame, I am taking the liberty of writing to you following our encounter the other evening.

I believe it is to you—do forgive me for not being sure—that I sent, centuries ago, a message. If this is true and you remember it, I beg your pardon. It was a thoughtless, silly, immature gesture and I didn't believe a word I was saying. The other evening I did realize this as soon as I saw you sitting there, you are not the woman I thought you were. Yours very theatrically, no, Yours very truly, no, very sincerely, no. Sincerely yours, T.

This letter does not seem convincing to T. He can't manage to write to this lady. It gets on his nerves and he finally writes: Madame, I am taking the liberty of writing to you, since we ran into each other at the theatre bar the other evening. Seeing you suddenly reminded me of an old forgotten affair. I should have written to you to make things clear a long time ago but I had forgotten your name and it's such an old story. Today I would like to apologize nonetheless for a letter I sent you ages ago. Perhaps you have forgotten it but it seems important to me to state this clearly: that letter was not intended for you and I don't know how I ended up sending it to you. I switched envelopes and caused what was meant for another to fall into your hands. Besides, it doesn't really matter, since in the absence of an answer I supposed that the mistake was obvious. So I thank you for that and conclude by sending you, Madame, my best wishes, no my very best wishes, no my most embarrassed wishes, no my respects, all right, Yours very sincerely, T.

There, it's done. T reads his letter over. So that lady will finally know it was all imaginary and she owes T nothing. He finds her address and goes to the post office. He stands there in front of the letterbox, he's preventing customers from posting their letters. A short breath and the letter is in the letterbox. The box is already full of envelopes, his falls on top of the heap, which reassures T a bit. If he changes his mind, he'll be able to retrieve it by slipping his fingers inside the letterbox. Yes, even with pudgy fingers, he sees he can grab it. T goes back to the theatre quickly, it's time to act.

LETTERS ARE NEVER WHAT YOU THINK, they do not keep their promises. They look full, but once opened, they are flat. Efina does not inspect the envelope before she tears it open. She doesn't think about the stamp, she doesn't look at the handwriting, she opens the envelope, and in her hand, T's handwriting. She reads T over and over. She thinks it's a mirage. She tells herself he's making fun of her and she'll go strangle him. Yes, she'll walk into the dressing rooms, drive out the actresses, make the girls run out of there and alone with T in his dressing room she will make him confess, she will make him spit out that what he wrote was not true at all: he made a mistake, the first letter was not for her, he mixed up two addresses. Besides, that doesn't hold water. Efina is stupefied. T wrote to her out of vengeance. He can't stop thinking about her and yet the letter was sent centuries ago. It's love, that's obvious, it can't be anything else. If not, why think about it still. Love, too late, Efina has put it behind her, she doesn't feel anything for T any more. But out of politeness, yes, out of consideration, respect for the man of the theatre, even if she has grown away from him, he still deserves an answer. She must write, it's her duty.

Her words run over the paper. T, she writes, Yes, it's actually me writing to you, although, since the beginning of time, I had forgotten you. I had lost you completely, and then to my surprise, I found you again the other night. I must say you've changed.

What the years have stolen from you I won't say, you can see it in your mirror and, considering your profession, it must be really terrible for you. I also think the stage has made you forget certain things which exist in ordinary life. Things like diplomacy. Tact. Like love of truth. Or honesty. Grace. I won't dwell on it. I know that you actors lose all sense of life and often act as if you were on stage. And yes, you are theatrical, you act out your dramas on stage, you make people laugh and cry and meanwhile you forget that people are flesh and bones and feelings go deep and hurt. For you life is a game. It is high time you settled back into this world of mine. Stop thinking of the past and all that childishness. Do you really think a letter sent by mistake could hurt. You are sentimental. You may be immature, but as for me, I am a woman used to the ups and downs of life. I am inured to them and you should know that the pieces of paper which often fall into my letterbox are of no importance to me. If there was a letter, I do not know. I have received dozens of them. Men wrote to me. I am not romantic, I peel vegetables on their letters and throw the whole thing into the rubbish. So don't worry. Paper cannot harm me. Let me add, since I have the chance, that you are a good actor, but be careful about your looks or soon you'll only get parts playing old fogies. I'll let you go now and I think it's time to say farewell. I wish you all the best for the future. Efina.

Efina reads her letter over and falls laughing onto her bed. But still, there were these words in T's letter: I would like to apologize . . . That sentence does require an answer. She picks up another piece of paper.

Dear Sir, she begins, I quite understand your desire to apologize, since that letter from long ago seems to torment you. It must have been important, for you to keep it in your head despite the passage of years. But it's my turn to tell you not to worry about it. I received nothing from you, I'm sure of it, and you can now sleep soundly. Cordially yours, Efina. Postscript: Would it be too inquisitive of me to ask you what that letter contained. I am indeed an admirer of your acting talent and I wonder what a man like you could possibly write a woman in a letter. Yours cordially again, Efina.

The answer immediately arrives. Efina receives an envelope that has T's writing on it. Dear Madame, I thank you for your understanding and I'm sorry if I have bothered you. Things are over then and I am quite pleased. As far as your request goes, I cannot answer you today, all that happened at least two ice ages ago and even if I remembered, I would be embarrassed to reveal to you words I wrote for someone else. Best wishes to you as well, Cordially yours, T.

Efina sends back an envelope: My Dear Sir, Pardon me if I insist. It so happens that I now feel implicated in this affair, since you have involved me in it. I am a romantic, I watch films, and the adventure of that letter piqued my curiosity. Allow me to insist: why were you writing that letter. Was it a love letter. Was it written to a woman with whom you were having a relationship. Yours cordially always, and with my sympathy, Efina. Postscript: I saw you perform Tuesday evening. You are tremendously talented. I noticed that you stumbled over the pronunciation of that English name that comes back six times in the play. Be careful not to make mistakes, if I may say so. Especially in the last act.

Madame, The woman to whom I was writing was only important to me for a short while. Three weeks perhaps, perhaps fewer. To tell the truth, I no longer know who she is or what her name is. I think she has changed a great deal and has become minuscule. She was a woman I was asking for a favour. I beg you now to forgive me if I break off this correspondence, I have a very demanding job, you know that, and a large family. I am a father, from several unions, and my youngest child doesn't go to school yet. Best wishes and friendly greetings, T.

Dear Sir, I know very well what it means to support a family. I myself have a child whom I raise alone and a dog who must be walked. But still, I must insist. It so happens that I know many people and I suppose I could help you in your quest for your friend. Just tell me a few things. Did she have dark hair. Was she short or tall. Were you very much in love. Did she answer you. In the hopes you have succeeded in correcting that little mistake in pronunciation, My heartfelt wishes to you, Efina.

Madame, Thank you for your corrections. I repeat: I wish to end this correspondence. That friend was not a girlfriend and she left my life as soon as she entered it. All that is absolutely unimportant. It was silly of me to have told you about it. I do not know if she had dark hair, I never noticed. I think there was an answer but it was insignificant and I forgot it very quickly. Besides, I was merely asking for a favour and there was no love, not one atom of it, in my letter. If you want an autograph, do drop by the theatre one evening. We're playing through next month. With my respects and in all friendliness, T.

Dear Sir, I wonder what that woman could have answered in her letter. I tell myself she was sincere but probably awkward, she was perhaps one of those people who lack daring and who fail every step of the way. Did she refuse to see you. Was she hard or nasty. What words did she use. Have you kept her prose. By the way, do you keep your correspondence. I keep everything, even postcards. I hope you are well and taking advantage of the fine weather, Efina.

Dear Madame, I don't have much time and cannot take an interest in what you are discussing here. You may be right when you suggest that this lady was not particularly pleasant. She was probably impolite and no doubt in a hurry when she produced her reply. There's a rather decent film on TV tonight, quite late, though. I'm sure you would like it. It's a sentimental story of the Russian kind. Sincerely, T.

Dear Sir, Thank you for suggesting the film. I watched it to the end and found it a bit simplistic. To return to your story, I wonder if in the letter your words were not ambiguous. Were your intentions clear? Would you perhaps have used terms which might have led someone to believe something. Would you have inadvertently declared your flame. Sometimes fires smoulder under words. I'm saying this off the top of my head as I seek to understand how that woman could have been dishonest or cold to you. My very best to you, Efina.

Dear Madame, I must tell you again that you are utterly mistaken. My intention was clear. My vocabulary was precise. I had only one thing to request. One cannot do very much, unfortunately, against nymphomaniac tendencies. In any case, I have forgotten. That lady went out of my mind and I would thank you for not putting her back in. All that happened at a time when I was still young and pink. When we both were, I should say, for if I remember correctly, you too show your age. Just between us, if I may say so, you should give up wearing those sports shoes, comfortable no doubt but they really lack class and do a disservice to your appearance. With all best wishes too, T.

Dear Mr. T, Thank you for your advice. Both of us are not so young any more and since you dare to be frank, I'm going to say it straight out: I think you're not sincere and there must be something you're blaming yourself for since you're still thinking about that woman. Did you love her, yes or no. You loved her of course. Efina.

Efina, What you are asking leaves me dumbfounded. Do you really think I remember feelings I had thirty generations ago. Just think that I have contracted three and a half unions in my life and if one supposes that in the intervals I was not living in the middle of nowhere, you will easily understand that the list of the women I've dreamt about is rather long. Of those I have cuddled. Of those I have admired, pampered. Of those I found beautiful and to whom I made love well. I can understand your attachment to your nice little tale. You are still young, you are alone, it does not surprise me that you try to experience affairs and passions, even if they happen to others. Best wishes and flatly yours, T.

Dear Sir, Excuse me if for a moment I thought you had feelings. I had forgotten the milieu in which you live and what theatre people are like. They are inconstant and flighty. They can one day write letters and sincerely deny them later. They are used to tinkering with stories any way they like. If they don't like them, they change them. They are used to disposing of their costumes every three months. I'm not surprised that you should change partners so often, nor that you have no problem in denying the obvious. And now I leave you to your stage. Learn your scripts by heart and don't forget to serve them up to your conquests at the first occasion. Good luck, Efina.

It's over. Efina goes to post her letter and she takes out the dog at the same time. She does not feel sadness. She does not need to cry, her eyes are absolutely dry. She is empty and frozen, she's just out of an ice tray. Her stiff muscles are saying that the affair with T is completely over. A few letters and an affair is forever buried.

A FEW LIGHT YEARS LATER, Efina meets a young man. Her child has grown and she pays babysitters from time to time when she goes out. She meets the boy at someone's place. He's younger than she, which Efina finds charming. She grows younger in his arms. She loves his voice and what he thinks. The other thing she loves, and does not say, is that he works in the theatre. He's a director. Yes, the boy she loves works as a director. There is nothing surprising in this, Efina has always been interested in the theatre. The boy puts on many plays and he knows all the actors in the world of the theatre. So, no wonder that what Efina deeply desires somehow happens: he picks T to act in a play. It is a repertory play, with a dozen parts. The boy hesitated, but ended up choosing T, not for the lead, for T can no longer play leading men. T's hairline has receded and this bothers him, you can see it by his way of brushing his hand over his skull. That's what Efina tells herself the day she sees him again. She does not wish to see T again, but since she's the boy's girlfriend, she's obliged to be there, especially at premieres, and she comes by to pick him up after rehearsals. In fact, she's coming tonight. The actors are at work when Efina enters the hall. She indicates that she's going to wait and she sits down in a corner. The boy is blocking out a scene with the actors. But T has to look at his pages, he doesn't know his lines and the director is growing impatient. Then they all scatter and the boy kisses Efina. She is merry, she laughs going down the stairs.

Another time, T and Efina find themselves alone in the theatre. The boy got a phone call during the rehearsal and he walked out to talk. The other actors have a day off, T is rehearsing a monologue. Efina enters the room where he's standing. The room is cold, there is no heat under the unpolished glass ceiling. In the middle of the room, T is sitting in a worn leather armchair coming apart at the seams, with his elbows on his knees and his hands folded in front of him. He answers Efina's greeting almost without moving his head and points to the director with his chin. Efina waits. Luckily she's wearing that dress, she paces the room and the fabric swings round her legs. Her arms are crossed because of the cold and under them her jacket moulds her torso. But T is not looking. His head is bent towards the floor. Efina walks nervously round. From time to time she throws in a word, a whisper to say: it's cold. T does not raise his head. She can contemplate his fat back. The back of his neck withered and wrinkled. Efina opens her mouth and words hatch in a vacuum. Without thinking,

34

she speaks like an actress. She asks for an explanation. As if he were her acting partner, she speaks to T without an introduction. She pretends to strip herself naked so T can bare himself to her. The skein comes undone. Months and years unravelled. Envelopes opened and glued. Letters unfolded and read. The whiteness of the very first sheet of paper oscillates far in the background. The word is found: feelings. T gazes upwards. She's standing in front of him. T's brow is knitted because his eyebrows are raised. He does not know what to answer. He is slow. He cannot find his lines. Two blurred words come out of his mouth. Terribly fatigued. A pitiful man. The director returns and puts his arms round Efina, toppling with her onto the armrest of the second armchair. These arms round her body are made of a foreign substance. Plastic. Arms, and a mouth.

The evening of the premiere. Efina fills her plate at the buffet. Just one seat left at the table, not far from T. He's talking and eating. He eats without refinement. A chicken wing is in his hand. He drinks without wiping his mouth. He wipes his fingers on his thigh. For what reason does T not think of using his napkin, that's what Efina wonders while she seems to be serenely tasting her meal. T's lips are greasy. Some women are not disgusted. Some women sometimes kiss T. He talks, he eats. He talks to someone to his right, she talks to someone at her left. She can't hear very well. T is making a speech about women.

T IS GETTING DIVORCED AND has lots of problems. Money problems, back problems, child problems and housing problems. It was stupid of him to have flirted with the young actress. He's not even remotely in love. She's skinny, her face is dark. He has to concentrate when he wants to say her first name. He remains silent when he's with her, they find nothing to say to each other. She smokes light cigarettes and her hair quickly becomes greasy. The skin of a Spanish woman, T thought every time he felt that rough skin against his nose. He didn't like her looks. Moreover, they only went to bed twice. It was surely too easy, he doesn't know why, out of habit. It's your midlife crisis, shouted his wife throwing the dishes on the floor and commanding him to choose. T didn't know what he was saying any more, he was tired, and instead of consoling her, he stepped out onto the street. He shouldn't have stayed out long, he should have come back at night instead of sleeping over at those people's place, and when he got back, the lock no longer recognized his key. He slept at other people's places and the lawyer's letters turned up in his hands. Then he didn't see his son much any more and his eldest children came to lecture him.

T is living in a hotel. His room is dingy. He's out of work. He thinks resentfully of the hotel rooms they stay in when they're on tour. They weren't always great but they had a bathroom. T has to piss in the bathroom in the hall. The whole hotel can hear him relieving himself. He no longer shaves every day and doesn't do his laundry. He looks like a part he played when he was young. The part of a decadent Hercules. He can see it in the mirror and in the street he exaggerates it, pushes it further. Either you are an actor or you're not; he laughs as he sees people turning their eyes the other way. To keep busy he scribbles in a notebook. His texts take the form of messages addressed to a certain woman. A lady who could be any woman.

Dear Madame, he writes, How are you this morning. I miss your face and your ill nature. I miss not knowing what silly things you're turning over and over in your head. You found a young man after your own taste. May you be satisfied with him. If not, come knock on my door here, my room is in the Hôtel du Bord, number forty-three. I will give you a hand. You are extremely scatterbrained. You believe everything people tell you and you are incapable of reading properly between the lines. You don't understand men, you just don't get it. I don't know how you live or how you can stand on your own legs. Look at the state I'm in—life has reduced me to this. I hold you largely responsible for the state I see myself in, inside this room. I have become an old jerk. I have been forgotten and the stage will perhaps never see me again. I can't even drown my sorrows in alcohol. I have always been a healthy man. I think I would have had a fine career, I would have succeeded in Paris if I had not received exactly at that moment a certain surgical wound. I was only able to get cured after a long, long time. Dear Madame, do you really think I can't tell that you're still sighing after me. Your life is not important. The only thing that matters for you would be to get immersed in my eyes. You go through life as if it were merely paper. And you think I would have the strength to carry you and keep you upright, give you thickness and breadth. I lack strength, dear Madame, I'm the one who needed it. If you had given me that, life would have held out its arms to me. You did not give it to me. We move forward like two ghosts, we are both pumped full of air and always on the verge of flying into the sky. Perhaps this is what connects us: that faculty of being here and absent at the same time. I spend my life writing to you and that's the thing I've done most seriously. When I'm with my family, when I rehearse, I have always been a bit distant. But thinking of you and writing to you, I have a feeling that my body is taking on weight. My letters fill up notebooks and writing pads. I suspect the women who share my life and my children and my cleaning ladies of having read and reread them as the years went by. It is, for me, the only way of explaining to myself why they've kept me near them and can still stand me. My letters fill up a good deal of space. I'm thinking of publishing them. I would like to show publishing houses what I am capable of. I think there will be some interest in this. A fine chunk of life, or I know nothing about books. Dear Madame, my wrist feels tired, I am writing by hand and, in addition, my back hurts, for I am writing stretched out on my bed, my elbows are sinking into the springs, they squeak endlessly every night. It bothers me that I did not succeed in revealing my prose to you. Things must get brighter. I am truly tired. Yours truly from this revolting grey room, the talented actor whom you admired, now, thanks to you, pathetic, in other words, T.

Out of his purgatory, T has been taken back into the residence of his ex. Women have the capacity of letting bygones be bygones. Back, but under certain conditions. There is some kind of curfew and if T is not back at the time hens go to sleep, the lock might well reject his key again. T would of course rather sleep with the little chicks, but he agrees to try and, if he spends the day running round while his wife is at work, it's all right with him to stay with her on her couch in the evening. At least he has agreed to try.

T GOES INTO A CAFE AND EFINA is having coffee at a table. The only people in the place are her and an

Italian waiter. The other tables have been set with tablecloths for lunch. It's the end of the morning. Both are extremely uncomfortable. They say hello and T has no choice but to sit down at that table. It's the only one that has no tablecloth, no napkins, no glasses. Efina smiles and says there's no such thing as chance but T believes there is such a thing as chance, so they have something to get their teeth into and don't have to be embarrassed as they scrutinize and examine each other. Efina has dark circles under her eyes. Her face of course has hollowed out and she has wrinkles but T recognizes the woman he met before the Big Bang. She puts her hand on her ear as she speaks, as if she didn't want to hear him or as if she were talking to herself. Her hand is dry and reddened. A hand that does dishes. It's a hand that must do work, yet Efina does not have a manual job. T thinks she's nervous and bustles about the house to work off tensions. Or else this woman is compulsive and spends her time scrubbing. Efina with a broom. Efina scrubbing the bathtub. Efina with the vacuum cleaner hunting down balls of fluff under the bed. Efina in a garter belt on the bed. Efina asks him where he lives and he's glad to be able to say that he's now living at his wife's.

She is somewhat surprised, for she'd heard that T was getting divorced, but she doesn't let him see it and to find out if he was lying, she asks all kinds of questions: how's his youngest. What kind of day care, what school. Is it a big house. Is it quiet. She refrains from being sarcastic and does not ask which wife he's living with now, there were so many in this man's life.

T takes advantage of these questions to ask her about her director boyfriend. He knows perfectly well as does everyone else that the boy is now going out with an Egyptian actress, but he wants to hear it from Efina's mouth and see her face when she says it. Efina says the boy no longer means anything to her and, besides, that relationship was unhealthy and Efina can now admit that he was not the man for her and the end of that affair was viscerally liberating. She takes advantage of this to imply that many men are after her and she's a much sought-after woman. A woman men fall in love with at first sight. A very attractive woman, in other words. She doesn't say this directly, she even suggests modestly that she can't understand why on earth she receives so many propositions. So many occasions. At her age. There is no explanation. Men are sometimes strange. T picks up on that: Yes, men sometimes are bizarre. But Efina should know that she has certain things going for her. Really, laughs Efina, T is truly very kind, she didn't know he was so nice, but she's mistrustful, for it is well known that T is a Don Juan. That's just it, says T, he has a little bit of experience and he can say that Efina has something about her that attracts men. Yes, he can see what is seductive in her person, even if she is slightly withered and even if she doesn't do herself up very well. Efina pretends to laugh but she's hurt and answers that she doesn't do herself up at all, she doesn't give a hoot, but this is not true, she needs more than an hour in the bathroom every morning. T gives her some advice on the way to dress, on the mistakes women make and things to avoid. The waiter would like them to pay now, it's the end of his shift. T struggles to find his change and she's the one who pays for the coffee. T protests but he doesn't have a cent in his pocket. Efina guesses this and asks if he's broke. T is surprised. He apologizes. He hopes she didn't think he thought she isn't pretty. On the contrary, he would like to say Efina is constantly lovely, he must say that it is rather rare for a woman to last with such steadfastness and that she's one of those women whose looks, when he thinks of it, astounds him. Efina takes advantage of this to say that it's impossible, since they never see each other. How could he think of her. For her, it's possible, she can applaud him on stage and every time, she must say, she's carried away by his acting. Often he is close to genius. As for him, it is quite impossible, there are so many young and interesting women round T. She knows he doesn't think about her. T has to respond on the contrary. He repeats that Efina is one of the women who has followed him through the years. It so happens there are faces that follow you all your life and Efina, even if she doesn't know it, has one of the faces that matter in his. Efina then asks him, does she really matter in his life. She does, T repeats, yes. Efina says that's absurd and she doesn't understand a thing and T answers that's the way it is, she's always on his mind. She never leaves his brain.

Efina is speechless, and after a rather long silence during which he clears his throat and runs both hands through his hair, T says he realizes that for her, this is hard to understand. Since for her, that's not the way it is. For her, he's just a performer. Certainly an actor she admires, an actor whose

44

talent she can see, and besides he thanks her for following his career so closely. But he is well aware
that for her the man behind the actor is not important. The most important thing is, naturally, what
happens on stage, and when the lights go out,
everyone goes home and turns away from the man
who carries the part on his shoulders. T's voice is
bitter when he says this and Efina touches his arm
above the elbow: now now, why is he saying that.
Perhaps she's not like the others, for on the contrary,
she has to force herself not to think of the man
breathing under the costume. She must force herself
because she knows he's not there for the women in
the audience. It's the character who's there for the
women in the audience, but what happens off the
stage, what the man does apart from acting, must
not be taken from him, must remain his secret. T
laughs, there is no secret; actors are normal people,
who eat, who sleep, suffer and love. He looks into
Efina's eyes. Efina takes T's hand. The hands of T
and Efina unite and play on the table. They no
longer dare look at each other and they stare at their
hands at play. Efina is thinking that T is a Don Juan,
she's naive, he does this with all women. T really
wants Efina and is afraid it shows. He releases her

hand and Efina, disappointed, thinks T is changing his mind and just wanted to have a little fun. They look at each other and they laugh. A really embarrassed laugh. Their hands feel orphaned, they want to get back together but they don't know how. Efina is afraid it's all over and she takes T's hand, which he had intentionally left on the table, back in her own. She leans over, so T's head won't be far from hers. She hopes T will dare. He takes his time. Then he dares. He leans forward and puts his lips on Efina's mouth. Efina's lips open, T is kissing her. T's tongue in her mouth. A short, solid tongue. A muscle like a snail. T says words that Efina never thought she'd hear, hear from T's mouth, for they are the same she's heard from other mouths. Everything is always the same. But this time, it's T's mouth. His voice, his tongue coming back like a snail. It's incredible how you can get used to things, how you get attached so rapidly—suddenly there are things you can no longer stop. Things that come back again and again. Movements that grow broader and gestures that are larger than what you would have predicted. T's hands on the nape of her neck. T's hands on her back. In her hair T's fingers. Efina's breasts are solid, that's a pleasant surprise,

T is always afraid that women's breasts might go flat and disappear under his palms. It is perhaps better to leave, the waiter is pretending nothing's going on but there are already customers sitting at other tables. No one seems to see T with his head lowered closing his coat and no one watches Efina leaving, hidden in her hair. But everyone has seen the couple's embarrassment, everyone knows where the hands went and exactly what path they took on the cloth. The diners know which portions of skin were caressed and which were not. All of them followed the kisses. The customers are thinking those two couldn't hold themselves back any more, they must have gone off to bed. A kind of regret is floating in the room, and mockery in their eyes when Efina returns hastily because she forgot her handbag.

THE GREATEST PROBLEM FOR A WOMAN who makes love in winter in a hotel room is the cold. T has licked Efina's body from top to bottom and the saliva is cooling as it dries. He turned Efina over eight times like a pancake. He grabbed her by the nape of the neck. He rubbed against her and his breath—she did not want to notice this—was not fresh. She did not want to notice that his body was flabby, his whole body was so flabby, practically no part could become hard. She did not want to notice that he was not wearing cologne and she heard nothing when he went to urinate loudly in the bathroom. Or that she didn't hear the toilet flush. Efina holds on to her dream. Still, she is a bit disappointed that T can't handle the latex and make it hold and that she'd had to go down and get it herself at the hotel office.

At this time of day, you don't meet anyone in the hotel. A coin in the dispenser and the package falls to the floor. Efina gets out of the way to let a cleaning woman and a trolley go by, then walks back up to number fifteen. T is standing at the window and Efina smiles at him to reignite what was born in the cafe. T smiles and the embarrassment thickens, because that thing is already dead. But Efina puts her arms round T and they lie down on the bed. It's easier to end things than to interrupt them and T whispers words that sound tender between the sheets. Efina pretends to be moved. Then T licks Efina from top to bottom and turns her over like a pancake. He rubs up against her and

Efina does not want to feel how flabby he is. How he toils and strains. She thinks of the condoms and asks would he have some in his bag by any chance. T answers that he doesn't have a bag. He has nothing in his pockets either. No condom in his pockets. And besides, he doesn't want any. That's what T proudly proclaims: he doesn't use those things. Efina is dumbfounded. If she could, she would even be angry and get dressed on the spot, but today is the day she's in a bedroom with T. She has dreamt for ages of being in this bedroom with T and she can only think it's exceptional, being in a bedroom with T. She goes down to the office. Meanwhile, at the window, T is getting tired in advance of what he must do and without realizing it, he's glad the whole thing will soon be behind him.

The latex does not want to hold. His member does not want to enter. T loses his temper—are these thingies for dwarves or what. But things must be pushed through to the end and T turns Efina over again a few times like a pancake, then lies on her, and in Efina's head boredom inevitably takes over, she waits and she's relieved when T finally releases. T is offended that Efina has not been satisfied. He would like to make her scream but Efina pushes him away and they remain lying there for a little while. She thinks of the very first letter. She hears two crows caw and a bell tolls shrilly twice. It's two o'clock, says Efina.

SHE HEARS ABOUT T FROM TIME TO TIME. Her interest has faded and she doesn't go to the theatre any more. A few days after the episode at the hotel, she received several letters and sent some, too.

Here is what the first letter said: Efina, We parted very quickly on the pavement the day before yesterday and I thought of sending you this sign of my friendship again. Not that I was particularly upset by that episode. We both know that these things can happen between women and men and from time to time they're not as rosy and beautiful as we might have hoped. Let's leave that aside, we are both adults and both of us have spouses with whom we manage to perform brilliantly at the top of our form. The marriage of bodies is a delicate alchemy and it is not rare that it does not correspond to what the minds want. Minds never stop fantasizing and when they lie down in beds, they often have surprises. We've both experienced this at least forty-six times, let's not waste time on it. I wanted to tell you that I hope you find love in life, if this has not already happened. You'll see that it can fulfil you and transform you into an eternally satisfied lover. I wish this for you with all my heart. T.

Dear Sir, answered Efina the very same evening, I should have expected your letter, for I should know what you're like by now. You never had the strength to admit things and you turn reality into whatever suits you. Now read my version instead: I too was rather disappointed by what happened between us. I confess I had expected more passion from you. You play brave men on stage but you're fearful in life. You have to admit that making love with a woman who is still young and beautiful, a woman you've desired all your life, blocked you completely and, if I may say so, took the wind out of your sails. Admit that you did not have the strength to summon all your energy to give both of us what we both desired since the day we were born. You preferred to play the older man, a weakling. Once again you were acting. You preferred to spoil everything. You preferred to hide behind a piece of latex. You did not dare to feel what my body was telling you and you wanted to think of nothing while you were penetrating me. I am angry with what you are and I'm sorry I wasted thoughts on a man who was not worth it. I still have, I hope, three or four decades left to live. I do hope I can purge myself of you and think of other, more sincere men. Condolences, Efina.

T's reaction arrives right away: Dear Efina, I can understand your violence. Being unsatisfied can lead to such a state. It must be difficult, and I repeat that I hope you very quickly find a lover who can lead you to fulfilment. In spite of that I thank you for your letter. As I read it on the bus certain facts appeared to me. It became crystal clear to me that no one knows us like our women. Our most intimate friends have no idea what we are like in bed. What we do with the flesh and how we manage it. Whether we are generous or bashful. In the midst of those women on the bus, with their shopping bags and their children, a feeling of tenderness came over me that I wanted to share. Do allow me to share that feeling with you and consider it as a token of my friendship, which is something, after all. All yours, with the hope that you'll be able someday to leave this bad patch behind you, T.

Efina

Efina is about to explode. T, she writes, you're even worse than I thought. Actually I feel sorry for you and pity you for still being like that at your age. You should see a psychiatrist. I can send you to a friend, her office is on rue du Creux, she's excellent and it seems she gets good results. Even with the toughest cases. I fail to understand what compels you to keep after me in this way. Either you do not love me and in that case don't write me. Or we are still connected and that's why you persist in sending me your prose. Nasty prose, may I add. I hope everything is fine with you and I, too, hope you will find peace of mind. Efina.

The exchanges are coming to an end: Efina, writes T for the very last time, Once again you are right. It is stupid of me to write to you since you are not dear to me. I wrote you a few letters, thinking it would please you and also in remembrance of the little we had shared. But you are less sentimental and since you're asking, I won't write any more. As for you, you may of course continue to do so. I will always read you benevolently despite everything. Yours truly, my best to you, and all good wishes for the future and for the rest of your life, T.

T'S LIFE ISN'T GOING VERY WELL. For one thing, there's the theatre: the economic situation is bad and fewer plays are being produced. T demonstrated on the street with people in his profession, but who cares about performers, the demonstration fizzled out and the whole thing ended up in cafes. T is not often hired, long are the weeks of unemployment. And then, there's that business with women. He doesn't know what's happening, he has almost no libido any more and, at the same time, he persists in picking up women, waitresses, passers-by, admirers, everyone he can. Which often puts him in the situation of finding himself in bed with a cumbersome lady he has no use for. He gets out of it by falling asleep at the beginning of the preliminaries. The women wake him up a few times, then the gentle and patient ones end up sleeping with him and the bad-tempered ones leave the bedroom with a nasty word, sometimes in writing, which he keeps. Those are the ones he prefers. That way the coast is clear and he can go out at night again. He has become an insomniac. Sometimes, too, he's rude and asks the lady to leave the room and it ends badly. He doesn't know what gets into him, once the woman is in the bedroom he doesn't feel like doing anything any more. He likes women who resist and looks down on the ones who say yes. Often he's dirty on purpose, he doesn't wash his hair and he watches the women simper about in front of his big, grey, greasy head. He watches how women say yes when he has hardly gotten into the preliminaries. It has become really easy. T wonders if the world is not peopled by nurses. Nurses, night mums, camp followers, good Samaritans and nannies—cool hands volunteering to console him when he falters. They probably need it, T says to himself, for he's good at playing men who are sensitive and not in the best of health. And tyrannical, that goes without saying. All this absorbs T and annoys him at the same time, but it annoys the woman he has chosen to move in with even more. She demands explanations and T swears twenty times a day that she's the woman of his life and he never cheats on her, which actually is not false, he can't remember a single name and once he even approached the same woman several days in a row. The woman he lives with takes him at his word. She is flattered to house the ageing actor, her girlfriends question her and she talks about it at length. She does not reveal every detail, the dirty laundry littering the whole house, the snoring, the constant bad mood and the absences that last two or three nights in a row. She says she's very lucky and an artist gives a great deal of himself. Yes, a great deal, enormously. An artist gives so much of himself, it's quite natural to make a few adjustments.

When T runs away he doesn't drink as some people might think. Luckily, he never could handle alcohol. It must be his constitution. His body seems strong, but it is actually fragile. He's afraid his liver will kill him as it did his paternal grandfather. Or the spleen like his mum. Or the lung like his brother-in-law. Or colon cancer like one of his cousins. He worries about his organism. The doctor, however, tells him there's nothing wrong with him. He's not sick but he needs a healthier life. He must walk more. Sleep more and keep from smoking. And of course avoid alcohol. In that respect T is lucky, he doesn't smoke any more and he doesn't drink. When he runs away, he goes to a cafe and spends the night in a hotel. He sits on a bench in the park and watches the gardeners renew their bulbs. He looks at the dogs being walked, he takes an interest in these dogs and, since he keeps seeing them, he wonders what could be going on behind their eyes and how life looks to them. And that's how he sees Efina. He sees Efina in the park. She's walking a dog whose colour proclaims the thoroughbred. A dog with silvery glints and a retractable leash. T sees her from afar and sometimes he comes back to the park with that hope, some days he doesn't go there, precisely out of fear of meeting her. He was able to observe that she looks different. She wears skirts that come up to her knees. She is a bit more careful in her dress but the way she does her hair is not to her advantage. T thinks women of that age should no longer do their hair that way. He also noticed that she wears things with high heels. Yes, but Efina once again has not really understood the lesson: those thick-heeled shoes, that wide leather, really, she does look like a secretary. T will go speak to her one day. Yes, one day T will have to give her a course on how to dress. He sees her with a boy. Could this boy be her son. Efina perhaps has children. These are details he cannot retain and besides, he realizes, of this woman he knows next to nothing. He sees Efina walk by with a man on her arm. Aha, things look serious, says T to himself when he sees them kiss each other discreetly on the mouth and watches from his corner to see how things are going. He is pleased, Efina doesn't look particularly in love. Understandably. The man next to her is insignificant, no presence, no colour and next to him T's brilliance would eclipse him completely, because if there's one thing T knows, it's that he's charismatic as hell. Another time, he doesn't see her and that's only normal, it's pouring. T persists in remaining on the bench. The passers-by turn their heads because of the old homeless man. A woman offers him a sandwich. But T persists in remaining there, because a dog goes out even in the rain.

EFINA IS GOING OUT WITH A DENTIST. They have lived together for a few months. Then she leaves him for one of his friends who promises to be a great actor. Some time later, he leaves her and she consoles herself with a dark-haired man who picks her up in a restaurant. That relationship lasts six weeks and she then decides to take a trip, which throws men her way. She has three or four passing boyfriends and she comes back home determined never to commit herself again. A neighbour makes her change her mind and now she finds herself for the next two years settled in a love affair slimy as oil. Her child can't stand the neighbour and, after many long discussions, she leaves him and moves with her son into a four-and-a-half room flat with southern, northern and eastern exposure. The dog is still with her. When the first dog died, and when the second, third and fourth dogs died, she replaced them immediately with a puppy of the same breed and almost the same colour. Her dogs are all called Igor, it's no more complicated than that. And even if they don't have the same personality and may have different habits, Efina doesn't notice because she's not interested in animals and doesn't like dogs that much. She doesn't particularly like the walks. If she keeps a dog, it's because it is good to have someone to welcome her in the evening and when she gets out of bed in the morning. It is good to hear sighs beneath the table and, in front of the TV, to pet something warm and furry against her leg. But twice a week at the supermarket, Efina curses as she piles up the cans of meat at the register. She would love to have an autonomous dog who could feed himself and didn't lose his hairs. A dog who recycled his excrement, she thinks while he's depositing his business and the passers-by check to see if she's going to pick up the turd.

From time to time, when she's bored and feels down, when her son goes out and she doesn't have a meal to cook, she opens the shoeboxes where the letters are thrown every which way. She reads through three or four. Depending on the day, she gets annoyed or she laughs. Her eyes stare into space, she does not understand, no she does not understand what happened with T. To think they were in that room. To think they really did make love. Or whatever it was. The thick hands of that man had been on her hips. She can't understand how it is possible that all that could have happened between the walls of a fridge, whereas the thought of T this evening overwhelms her. Could she be attached to a man who has no reality. Could she have invented an image. After dozens of such reflections she resolves to undertake what she wanted to avoid. To write another missive. To meet T one last time and in the morning light, with rested mind and eyes, in the cold, neutral and bright light of a place of her own choosing, she will look at that man, she will listen to him talk and without prejudice, with a calm mind, she will decide if T is the man she thinks he is or if she blinded herself.

The letter is not easy to write. Efina has her pride and she still remembers the condescending note that T last sent. Dear Sir, she writes, then changes her mind: Dear T, You will be surprised to receive a letter again. I must say I'm equally surprised to be writing it. It so happens I would like to talk to you one last time. Perhaps you have no desire to do so and in that case I will leave you in peace. But perhaps you would nonetheless be good enough to come to the Grand Café Chiméri Thursday at ten in the morning. I will not keep you for hours. Hoping for an answer and sending you my cordial greetings, Efina.

She calls the theatre and they give her an address. She posts the letter but unfortunately this is one of those times T has run away and, besides, he doesn't read his post, it's his girlfriend who sorts the post and she throws the letter into the wastebasket. T gets letters from his female admirers from time to time and they are of no importance. Efina waits for the answer. Wednesday goes by and Thursday there is no letter in her box. She decides to go to the cafe. She waits until eleven. T does not show up.

Back home, she writes: Dear Sir, I know you are negligent but you could still have answered me in the name of our former friendship (put that word in quotation marks). I waited for you in vain. Thank you for reading this. Efina.

It so happens that this day T comes back home and his girlfriend has the letter in her hand. She asks him for an explanation. Who is this Madame Efina. What kind of friendship was it and why did T never mention it. Why did this lady make a date with him. T doesn't know, he reads the letter, he says it's a misunderstanding and he's going to answer the lady.

He takes out his writing pad: Dear Efina, I have just perused your letter. I can guess that you waited for me somewhere I did not go. I am back from a tour abroad and your invitation never reached me. You may be certain that otherwise I would have apologized. There may have been certain trying episodes in our past, certain difficulties, but believe me when I say I am neither ungrateful nor dishonest. Yours in friendship, T.

Efina is softened by these words. Dear Mr T, she writes, I had asked you if we could meet at the Grand Café Chiméri. Can you come next Thursday at ten. I have something to ask you and then I will bother you no more. All best, Efina.

EFINA CHOOSES THE TABLE with the best lighting. The one farthest from the door and farthest from the bar. The one with no table facing it. The one where two potted plants make a thin screen. She sits facing the door. No, better to sit on the other side, T will be in the light. No, that way she won't see him well, he'll have his back to the window. She changes seats another time. She chose to wear slacks and a deep-cut blouse. Her make-up is light and she hopes T will appreciate it. She did not risk perfume for fear that because of the conspicuous smell T might think her goal is to charm him. Her goal is quite different and she doesn't give a hoot if T is charmed. She checks her make-up with her pocket mirror anyway. She checks her eyebrows. She checks her cheeks. The blue eye shadow is impeccable and the cheeks discreetly pink. She's facing the clock and she follows the hands. Thirty minutes late, a lot for a normal person but it's nothing for someone like T. Certainly, when he arrives, he will not apologize, the word late is not in his repertoire.

The hands keep trotting away and T is now fifty minutes late. There are a few more people around and the waiter brought over a second cup of coffee. Efina needs to go to the bathroom but she doesn't dare, she doesn't want to miss T. If he comes while she's there and doesn't see her, he is capable of making an about-face without waiting. He's capable of not seeing her, that's why her eyes do not leave the door, she's ready to wave her arm and even ready to shout T, and God knows she hates to make heads turn. Her eyes go from the door to the clock. T decidedly is not coming. Efina makes a decision: if by eleven T is not there, she will get up, she will go to the toilet, she'll pay and that's it. At eleven o'clock she will get up. She will not wait one second more. The hand of the clock quivers and sets on eleven. Annoyed and frustrated, Efina gets up. She walks to the middle of the cafe. At that moment T comes in and makes all heads turn. He has his hat over his long grey hair. He's wearing his trench coat. He's wearing his narrow red scarf. He's massive and bent over and when he speaks, when his voice calls out: Efina, it is a theatrical voice. He makes a thousand excuses for being late and his words in the room sound like lines in a play.

Efina

Efina leads him to his seat. She wonders if T sees her. Did he examine her. Is he aware that she's sitting opposite him. He talks and talks, he's jovial, he tells all kinds of stories, he can't stop. One thick mass. Sometimes he asks questions but he leaves no room for answers. With some effort, Efina says: It's nice of you to be here. She wonders if that smell is actually coming from him or if it's from the direction of that potted plant. T grows silent and looks at her attentively. If only he could take off his hat so she could see his face better, she does not dare suggest it to him. With T in front of you, you never know what he's taking in of his surroundings. It's all those words he's projecting, you wonder if he can possibly perceive the world beyond. But when he's calm, on the contrary, you'd think he was walled in. She's talking now in front of that wall. She's shy. T's little eyes scrutinize her and she can't know what he's thinking, if he is there or even if he understands. She picks up her courage and she says what she had prepared: she's sorry for what happened. Was it a misunderstanding. Or was there really that thing with him, that had gone on for years now. T says nothing and Efina feels compelled to elaborate. This wasn't what had been planned. The plan was to stay calm, not to talk with emotion. Not to say serious things. Not to express feelings nor have tears come to the eyes nor have T put his hand on hers. T's hand is thick and warm. Efina laughs. She says here we go again and T smiles and there they are again. Their hands play together on the table. Efina says she's warning him, she won't go to a hotel any more and T laughs, he says he won't go either, things between them are platonic now and he leans forward and puts a kiss on her mouth. Efina smiles and T leans forward again. Efina is caught up in T's smell and in his lips. Things turn slightly less platonic. T's thick arms go round Efina's shoulders and she thinks she should be disgusted, given the look of his trench coat. And yet, no, she likes it. T's greasy, dirty hair is now against her cheek, T gets up heavily and sits down next to her. She's right up against him. She smells his odour and she laughs, she can't stop laughing while T says childish words of love in her ear. Every now and again T's lips move up and down her neck. On her earlobes. It is clumsy and charming. His thick hands immobilize her own, she feels all shut in. She can no longer move. She is shackled and delighted. Now T's right thigh comes to rest on her own. That thigh is rather heavy, but she does not dare protest. Her legs are pretty well crushed. T's hands are on her body. He's not very skilful but she's glad, she's back in his arms again. T whispers in her ear words she can't really grasp, he's doing it on purpose, it's because he's ashamed, he doesn't dare tell her what he's saying. He's excited, he wants to leave, they could kiss closer up.

Efina calls the waiter over, she pays. They leave like teenagers. T finds a not very discreet corner and thrusts his tongue into her mouth. T's tongue is mushy and still like a snail. He leans on her force-fully and kneads her buttocks with both hands. He vigorously rubs Efina's crotch, T's nose is in her neck, his sweaty cheek on her forehead, it's incred-ible how a man can sweat. There's a lady watching. Efina's bladder is burning, she really needs to go to the bathroom. T is wriggling round against Efina's body and she no longer feels very much like going on any more. Just for the whole thing to be over, perhaps. What she'd like is to sit down and talk but T continues for a while, he doesn't know how to get out of it, the thing they had recaptured has escaped again. At last he draws away from Efina. His hat is back on his hair. She's afraid he might be mad and she takes him by the arm. T stares at his feet on the ground. She tries to joke but T is not on her wavelength at all. He's in a rush. He must leave. He's already late. He must not be late. He has to be careful. He has to go *that* way. Efina has the bright idea of saying she hopes he's not going to write another one of those letters, his speciality. That makes T laugh, he gives Efina a hug.

FINALLY. THIS TIME EFINA IS IN LOVE for good. She's no longer bored under the blankets. The name of the prince charming is Raúl, he's tall, black, he's sensitive, intelligent, and Efina can be seen on his arm all over the city. T spots them a number of times in the park with the dog. He sees them in the theatre. Once he passes by them on the street. T knows that there is such a thing as chance but, good God, you'd think they were the only lovers in the city. Efina rediscovers that a body can be used in every conceivable way at the same time. A head can be used as a brush to polish what is between the legs. A nose can go into a sex. A sex can find pleasure in lodging under a knee. Squares of ticklish skin are placed everywhere on the body. A tongue thrust into an ear. Hands stroking the underside of the feet. A belly on her shoulder blades. Efina is in seventh heaven. Raúl takes up all her time. She thinks of him when he's not around. She sleeps with him. She leaves on holidays with him. She eats what he cooks for her, she listens to the music he likes and reads the books he recommends. This situation is well known and discussed round her. Some friends of hers are of the opinion that Efina should be careful and shouldn't let herself be completely invaded. She should keep a portion of secret garden for herself and not open the country from border to border as she does. Not be so wide open. Reflect and think for herself. Keep her tastes, her friends. Not always say yes to Raúl. Other friends on the contrary find what she's living through charming and would love to experience such total fusion. It's lovely to see them together. A handsome couple, Efina and Raúl. If only they could have children. They should start a family. A pity it's a little too late, Efina won't have any more children. And then, her son is living with his father.

Luckily they have the dog. Raúl and Efina spend hours laughing about the dog. Talking about his adventures. Getting him to run after his toys. They pick out cans for him and take him to the vet. Efina is happy that Raúl loves this animal. Not only does he love Efina but, on top of it all, he loves her dog. Raúl's love is total. He often gives her presents, on her birthday and St Valentine's Day, but Raúl is not so common, he also has surprises for her and he always manages to please her. Efina surely doesn't give as many presents to Raúl. To excuse herself she says that she has no imagination and she's too afraid to make a mistake. She's afraid of disappointing him. Occasionally she has given him things he didn't like. Things that left him stone cold. The black scarf, for instance. Or the waterproof cigar box. It is true that Raúl doesn't smoke, but the thing was cheap and if someone gives you a cigar, you have to have a place to store it. That's what Efina explained to Raúl. And also that she doesn't always know what he may want. She doesn't always quite understand his tastes. Yes, since she has occasionally made mistakes. Remember the belt. Think of the cufflinks. Recall the comic books. No, for her, it's better to avoid presents. She says she pampers him in other ways, she shows him love differently. Still, the cufflinks stay in a drawer now. They are never worn. They did cost a pretty penny. Efina thinks they would be perfect for T. She knows T would like them, she can't say how, but she knows: T likes cufflinks like these. Same for the black scarf. She knows T wears a scarf. She often saw that little scarf on him. So she knows with certainty that if T saw that scarf, he'd be thrilled to bits. If T saw the black scarf, the black scarf would be adopted right away, there wouldn't be those awkward moments like with Raúl, no silences and stiff thank-yous. No, with T there would be no thank-yous, but the scarf would go round his neck that very second. And it would stay there all winter long. And if Efina remembers correctly, T smoked on stage once. OK, maybe he didn't like it and maybe it was only for the play. Still, Efina knows T isn't that narrow-minded and may even consider smoking a little cigar someday. And the box would look good at T's. The idea grows in her head to give T the black scarf. To give him the cufflinks and the cigar box. She'd have to go about it the right way. Not rub T the wrong way. He mustn't feel obliged. She thinks of having a package delivered to the dressing rooms with a card, of the kind: From a woman who admires you. Or: From your friend, E. That way T couldn't return the package and Efina would have a chance of seeing the scarf round his neck someday. Yes, but what if T didn't want to accept an anonymous scarf and gave it to his sons. If T—he's very impulsive—gave it to the lighting technician. If T—he's so absent-minded—left it behind in one of the dressing rooms. If he lost it in a bar. No, T must know that the scarf comes from Efina and then he'll take care of it. Efina begins going to the theatre again. On her arm she carries a bag in which the black scarf is rolled. The scarf is bulky, she had to give up the idea of putting it in its netted pouch. Raúl gets bored at the theatre and tries to keep her with him in front of the TV. But Efina is inflexible. She has a passion for the theatre. She can't do without it any more. There's only one thing on her mind: give the black scarf to T.

It's not easy. First of all, T isn't seen very much on the stage any more. They say it's because he's famous. He harvested a lot of money. He can afford a breather, he can pick parts or turn them down at will. The truth is, T isn't much in demand any more. His stature is imposing, he has a leonine look. He is terribly charismatic. He has a weathered face. His face tells stories even before he opens his mouth. And his deep voice is legendary. T is a human monument. But T is also unpredictable. He isn't reliable at all any more. He doesn't show up for rehearsals. He doesn't always know his lines. He interferes with the director and treats the actors like children. He sleeps with the young actresses. Twice he made a big scene and had to be replaced. Or else he's prostrate, empty. No, really, directors don't feel like going through all that. They can't take chances, they're responsible for the whole production. So they hardly call T any more. Or at a pinch for scripts he records alone in radio studios. But what a pity, directors sometimes say when they meet in cafes. What a pity, say the make-up artists, stage managers and directors. We don't see T any more, says the public. But that's the way it is. T is a Titanic leaning towards the abyss and there's no help for it. There's no solution on earth. Or else you'd have to invent one.

Moreover, when T performs, he rarely shows up at the theatre bars. He doesn't like his admirers. When he was young, he spent entire evenings being praised to the skies in the foyers of theatres. But at the age he is now, with his experience of the trade and the laurels the critics have placed upon his brow, even in foreign languages, with the halo that surrounds his name when it comes up, he can allow himself to walk out of the theatre like any other employee. He leaves when the lights have hardly gone out. He walks out onto the street and what do you know, he looks like a regular guy. He goes to bed early or has a drink in a cafe. A drink all by himself, looking at the drunks. Listen to the drunks in bars, yes, they're the ones who really do theatre, that's where you find the real actors. T watches them ramble on with their speeches and monologues. He thinks of his past roles and so what. His profession is just cardboard. A man with a sandwich board, that's what he is. A profession that leaves you unsatisfied. You're always on the surface. You act, you die, what's left. Memories in people's minds. That's the reason actors are so eager for recognition. It's a profession that gives you nothing but hot air. Without fame their life would be hollow, it has to be filled up with praise. And T has had more than enough praise, more than he deserves, he has seen his face so much he's disgusted, in every newspaper of the country, crinkled and pimpled, as he says. He doesn't even pay attention any more. He hates the articles that mention him and looks down on the journalists who take time to write about him. Don't those people have any decency. Those people have no originality. They can't think of anything new to say. They moo along with the herd. They don't seek out what is fresh and new. No desire for purity. They like to marinate in the soup, a revolting thirty-year-old soup. But T knows himself by heart. He would like them to throw out the soup and talk about other people now. True, he's a great actor. True, he did some fine things. There are some fine memories. And now, what's left. He's with the drunks, he's having a drink.

BUT EFINA HANGS AROUND the foyer with her over-stuffed bag. T was hired to play in a big production. They need stage phenomena of his kind once in a while. The show is playing for a few weeks in this city. Efina returns to see the play a dozen times. The usherettes end up recognizing her and among themselves they call her the woman with the bag, or the secretary. She finally dared to ask questions about T and the usherettes understood the nature of this lady's passion for the theatre. And since they are also women and potentially in love, they do their best to inform Efina. They give her information and tell her when T, according to rumour, has arrived in the dressing rooms, more or less five minutes before the curtain rises. They tell her what's happening, as much as they can anyway, for the ushers have work to do. But from time to time, a messenger returning from backstage reports that T is there, that he's in fine form or, more often, in a terrible mood. That he smells or the actresses are complaining about him. That they don't know if he's going to perform, everybody is nervous and things backstage are on the verge of exploding.

Efina takes her seat in the theatre. Instead of admiring him, she's afraid it will all go off the rails, he'll begin to howl or he won't know his lines, afraid he'll have a huge blank and have to be committed immediately. She can see stretcher bearers come running. She sees the ambulance arriving. She hears the siren wailing and stopping on the pavement and the audience glued to their seats watching T's degradation. The role he's playing doesn't interest her. She knows he's wearing a suit with a cheap-looking jacket. He is grotesque and she resents the director for forcing him to look ridiculous. Luckily, they're all grotesque, from the first to the last, the cute little actress with half-visible nipples takes the prize. The audience leaving the theatre flock into the foyer. Efina has stationed herself at the actors' exit. Emergency exit, it says, over the door to the courtyard near the containers. There's a light bulb over it. Young men are coming out. The lover, the cousin and the one who played the naive character and made the audience laugh a lot. They're in a hurry. The bulb shows dull, preoccupied faces.

UNPLEASANT IDEAS ARE SPROUTING in T's brain. For some time now, people have been going on and on about that business with Efina and her foreigner. Those two are all you hear about. That magnificent, superb couple. T has had it with those two. On top of that, T keeps bumping into them. Chance can be malicious all right. Once, in the supermarket, T is standing with his purchases—in fact only a writing pad, because he doesn't do the cooking and would be incapable of taking care of a fridge. And who is standing there right in front of him. Efina, with her foreigner. The foreigner is carefully piling cans onto the belt. Oh you could see it was important, could see he was putting all his talent into it. T finds him effeminate and slightly overdressed. The kind of man who'd wear cologne and make appointments with the hairdresser. He is joking with the girl at the cash register. He is exchanging smiles and intimate words with Efina. At one point, Efina and he look at each other eye to eye and the foreigner asks, You're sure, about dinner. And Efina says, Of course. And we also have cheese. And T hates them. T tries to hide behind the other customers but he's not sure if Efina recognizes him in the queue. In any case, she is babbling away gaily, she is talking to her little darling and it won't bother her if the whole store overhears her. Thank you, goodbye, Efina and her man say, all smiles. The girl at the register is radiant and T irritably plunks his pad down on the belt. He fumbles through his pockets. He is missing ten cents and the cashier is not smiling. A lady lends T ten cents.

Another time, T sees them again in the park. He's already seen them a thousand times. They always come back to this park. There are loads of other parks but T comes back here too. He doesn't like their dog, by the way. A pedigreed dog, that's vulgar. A pedigree means: look at me, I'm loaded.

T can't understand how Efina can own a dog like that. To have a dog, yes, OK. But a mutt, a bastard. Not one of those animals that die of pneumonia because they went out in the rain. Not those aristocratic dogs, those thoroughbreds that cost you at the vet's. A mutt, yes, it's tough. It eats whatever garbage is lying round. It's rain-resistant. It sleeps wherever it can, wherever you want. Besides, T decides that if Efina's dog comes near him someday, if it dares sniff his bottom, if it sniffs his knees, we'll just see if T doesn't give it a good kick. But luckily, Efina's dog is cautious and does not go over to his bench, even when not on a leash.

Efina often sees T on that bench. She pities him because he looks more and more like a homeless man. Even Raúl has talked about him to her . . . that guy with grey hair in the park . . . At the same time she's pleased to know he's not too far away. She thinks he's looking for her. She thinks she can feel his eyes staring in her direction. She takes particular care how she dresses for the park. Raúl thinks she's being coquettish and it's not worth it, changing her skirt to take out the dog. Retrospectively, Efina is glad she didn't give him that scarf. That way T does not have to thank her. She could have found herself in a delicate situation: the old homeless guy who thanks her for Raúl's scarf. Raúl asking questions. And what about giving him the scarf when Raúl is with her. She could explain to Raúl that this man is an actor. He's a declining icon. She'd like to give him a present and the scarf in the drawer is useless in any case. We could do something nice and at the same time get rid of something. Raúl knows Efina's passion for the theatre, he won't be worried. And seeing the state T has fallen into, who could think that this man could arouse someone young, light, classy, pretty and feminine like her. No, Raúl won't be jealous. Efina and Raúl have been walking out in the park with the scarf for a few days now. But you'd think it's on purpose, Efina wonders if T isn't telepathic—now that she wants to speak to him, he has totally vanished. T no longer sits on that bench and after two weeks, she puts the scarf back in its place.

That absence worries her because she can't stop thinking about T again, over and over. Certainly there were relapses, especially with that scarf, but on the whole, since Raúl, Efina congratulated herself for almost never thinking about T. Almost never. No, hardly ever. OK, there were always times when her mind, off its leash, took advantage of its freedom to run off straight to T, but Efina called it back and she thinks she's making progress. She's no longer totally obsessed. She almost never rereads the letters. She has almost forgotten them. Sometimes she would even think of throwing them away. But for that, she's not quite ready. Speaking of letters, she wonders if she shouldn't write to him to ask where he's gone to. It's been weeks since he hasn't come to the park, after all. Of course actors go on tour, but she doesn't know why, she has the feeling T is not on tour. There are also holidays, but she's also sure T doesn't go away on holidays. Nor on trips. T has no family life.

At this time, Efina begins to receive letters. Letters of a kind no one likes, totally anonymous letters. They are posted from this city, in a distant neighbourhood. The letters are not nice and they make fun of Efina. What is more serious is that they accuse Raúl of being a foreigner. The tone is vulgar, but one can sense that the author is dissimulating a more refined pen. The trouble is, Efina recognizes that tone and style from the beginning. Yes, there are certain turns of phrase which Efina knows by heart.

She writes: Dear T, I have no idea where you are nor in what hole you've been hiding. What you are doing is idiotic. I recognized you right away, by your turns of phrase, and I recognized the paper: you always buy the same kind. I don't know what got into you, sending me this drivel. It must be a joke. You are naive if you think you could fool me. No one writes nowadays. You are the man who sent me the most letters in my whole life. The only letters I have ever read came out of your mouth, or almost. You might say I'm an expert in your corres-pondence. So stop this game. If you wish to speak to me or if you wish to see me, I go to the park every day. But you know that, don't you. Greetings nonetheless from your old friend, Efina. Postscript. I am glad to receive these signs from you anyway. For a moment I thought you'd kicked the bucket and I skimmed the obituaries.

And now, where to send that letter. She sends it to his last woman, the one who sheltered T for a long time. Two letters arrive the same day at Efina's

Efina

residence. One in the crude writing of the anonymous sender. The other in the messy writing of T.

Bitch, it says in the first letter. Dear Efina, says
the second, I have no idea what you're talking about
and what misdeed you are accusing me of, but how
nice to receive a little sign from you. If I were someone else and didn't know you, I would've been
angry when I read you. But I've known you for
centuries, I've been reading your prose since the
invention of the moon and I know you're always
getting your hackles up and you tend to be caustic
and cutting. Let me answer your postscript: no, I am
not deceased, but it is true that my health has suffered these last months. I'm writing from the hospital where I'm being treated for pneumonia. I spent
too much time recently dreaming alone in a park
and watching silly geese who walk their dogs with
their men. I think I wasn't able to stand it. And
that's what happened to me. I hope that you on the
other hand are in perfectly good health and flour-
ishing. Yours very truly, T. Postscript. Watch out
for menopause.

T, answers Efina, I'm sorry about your illness
and hope you will regain the little energy you had.

I myself had a narrow escape: I was spending a lot of time in a park pampering homeless vagabonds and I barely escaped that pneumonia. A healthy, virile man kept me in my room. With best wishes for your prompt recovery, Efina.

Efina is getting married. The decision was not easy. Raúl proposed but Efina couldn't bring herself to say yes. She didn't know what she wanted. She could neither say yes nor no. Thinking it over, she finds few faults in her man. She loves him with conviction. He's sensitive, deep and cultivated. He loves to cook. His ideas make sense. He's handsome and nice, children love him. He seems to be faithful. He would have wanted babies but that wasn't possible. He makes plans for the future and every evening tells her he loves her. Any other woman would say yes. But Efina doesn't know why, at that point she gets lost. What if Raúl wasn't the right man. And what if there were another one for her on this earth. What if the next day she were to meet someone different who—who what. What could another man offer her that Raúl does not possess. He has an exotic accent. He teaches her lots of things. He follows her on shopping expeditions. He introduces her to other people. You don't get bored with Raúl. He's sociable, he plays a musical instrument a little, he adores the dog, and tidying up their flat never bothers him. He's a perfectly fine lover. Yes, she likes her lover. He has proposed to her. Many of Efina's girlfriends say she's lucky. Raúl, the ideal fiancé. In the list of award-winning men of all Efina's girlfriends, Raúl takes first place. And there are no ties. Raúl wins the medal hands down.

Efina's in the dress. The white dress sculpts her torso and Efina's breasts are visible. Raúl is afraid the official won't reach the end of his speech. Efina is surrounded by friends. She feels feverish and she's trembling a little, that's only normal, it's the first time she's getting married. It was high time, say the friends, later she would have been old. And a bride who's too old spoils the whole thing. While Efina, despite some very discreet wrinkles, is radiant and can still fool people with the help of a little more make-up and time spent in the bathroom. Her son in a bow tie is on this day delightful. He refrains from attacking Raúl and says that he's almost a father to him and the guests shed a tear. It's a real shame that Efina should have these thoughts at her finest moment. Really, it's a shame, she's mad at herself, inside her she scolds and lashes herself. She orders herself to stop. Stop thinking of T now. Your fiancé is Raúl. Your man. Your Raúl for ever. But inside herself there's an eye telling of a wedding with T. A wedding where the fiancé is not handsome, tall and virile, but heavy, bald and stooped. A wedding where the bride-to-be looks lovingly at her fat toad of a fiancé. A wedding where the kisses make the children shriek with horror. A woman who is still young cannot kiss such a man. No, nature forbids it. Oh, it is truly unfortunate that at the moment of consent, the moment of kissing the husband and signing the papers, she should have on her mind only her T.

T.

T.

T.

That's how one can sabotage the best moments in life. That's how instead of being happy, a woman has to live in a state of unrest. That's how you can dance at your wedding as if it were a funeral. But the years of marriage with Raúl are happy. Efina has no complaints. No fighting. You have to think this is harmony. Except for that episode which shook them up a bit. The episode of the dog's death. The dog whose name was Igor, like his father and all his grandfathers. Well, that's a figure of speech, they were not from the same line, only from the same breeder. Efina was sorrowful but not like Raúl. His sorrow was frightening. Efina may mourn for a dog but the next day it's over. It's not the first dog she's lost and she knows they're replaceable. Of course each is unique. Each has its own personality. But going out for a walk, sniffing up walls and trees, raising its paw all the time and licking their bowl to the bottom, they're all the same and that's what Efina says. Raúl's opinion is different. That Igor was a person. He had a glint in his eye. Igor expressed himself in a way that no other dog can. Raúl claims he could grasp every nuance of his bark. Igor had a real personality. True, a canine personality. But he had qualities that could be named: playful, mercurial. Raúl says Igor at certain times had sulked but Efina can't believe him. Raúl says Igor was a helpful soul and if Raúl came home tired, Igor would leave him the couch. Efina hadn't noticed that either. Did she notice that Igor understood right away when Raúl was feeling sad. No, Efina did not know and she's especially worried that

Raúl may have felt sad. Did she notice that Igor came in every morning to encourage him while Raúl was shaving. Yes, Efina certainly did see that dog in the middle of the passage. Did she realize that Igor would always start with the peas in his dog food. And that peas gave him gas. And that he digested meat better. In the evening, he was often thirsty. And he'd almost managed to open the fridge all by himself. Raúl is mourning for Igor and forbids Efina to get another dog right away. Igor goes into the incinerator. They don't speak of the tragedy again, what's the point. It's better not to relive these things. It was no one's fault. You can't predict what might happen. A crazy dog, and the harm is done. Traffic is heavy in these streets. A dog who's not on a leash, but why wasn't he on his leash, no no no, let's not talk about it, what's the point, why stir things up. It was no one's fault. The driver couldn't have known. The dog couldn't have known either. He was in the wrong place. It's really too dumb, Igor didn't have any luck.

Raúl's recovery takes time. He can't understand how Efina can be merry and eat with such a hearty appetite. He can't swallow a thing, he's lost seven pounds. Efina doesn't understand either how you can get sick over a dog. There are so many dogs in the world. They should get another one fast and the vacuum will be filled. They'll be able to take walks in the park again. With, naturally, a leash. But this time she wonders if she doesn't want to change breeds. She's tired of that colour, she'd like a white dog. What does Raúl think. Raúl is in a bad mood. He stays on the couch and doesn't go to work. He makes an appointment with the doctor and eats two pills a day. He watches Efina moving about. Talking about trivial things. Those little things that make up ordinary happiness, like: who's going shopping. Or: what will we do this Sunday. We should change the curtains. And when are we going to repaint the bed-room. We'll buy a new mattress. And the box springs, this one creaks. It creaks, but it's not urgent. It creaks less and less often and Efina reads more and more books. The novels Efina reads have grown fat. When they first met, Efina didn't read in the evening. She would read Raúl's hands. Then Efina brought to bed books and magazines that spent the night with them. Now she's installing novels in the bed, she's mad about stories that take up several volumes into which she disappears com-pletely. Raúl only sees the top of her skull and he falls asleep with the light in his eyes. Raúl looks at Efina and discovers questions that had not yet come into his head. What is Efina thinking. Is Efina in love. Deep down in his wife, what is there. Raúl watches Efina becoming opaque and rough. But she seems to have a glint like Igor's in the back of her eyes. Raúl is happy with Efina. Of course you can always find better, but he really can't complain. A woman like her is not so common. Raúl's friends say so and in the list of prizewinners among the wives and partners of all Raúl's friends, Efina barely takes third place, tied with Misha's wife, the one with the great legs. Raúl sees life from a distance. He allowed himself to get closed in as if he were living in banana crates. He moved forward in life with flowers and fruit, but all that seems over and in this city it's as if he were contained in a few banana crates. It's neither hard nor bad but soft and bland. Walls the colour of banana crates. A banana-crate sky. Banana-crate thoughts and people.

EFINA AND RAÚL TAKE WALKS with Olaf. Olaf has a retractable leash but he's not allowed to go far, you never know what might happen. You never know what happens when dogs run off and Olaf is not allowed to distance himself from them. Just enough to raise his paw without having the leash pull his neck. Enough to sniff calves and buttocks, almost close enough to touch them. Just enough not to sniff up girls and get them pregnant. Olaf is a boy. Igor, you couldn't tell any more, Igor had been the recipient of a treatment related to his attributes. But Olaf is a handsome male, you can see that, people notice it. He has a long, slender muzzle. A narrow body, all muscle. Slim flanks, tight under his short, matte coat. He has a small bag of skin attached to his abdomen. There's nothing to criticize about him, Olaf is obedient. He might get into some mischief, he might run off at top speed or stick his nose into something dirty, but he's wise enough to turn round and warn you as soon as he gets the idea, so you can get hold of him and scold him before he commits the crime.

Olaf is not Igor. Igor had something more relaxed about him, a slightly looser skin that hung down in certain places: under the jaws, at the knees. Perhaps Igor was older. It's silly to say that, Igor is dead and Olaf is not living at the same time. Raúl was right: it seems Efina can notice a difference between Olaf's bark and Igor's bark. Igor's had some substance in it, something like hoarseness. A chunk caught in the voice. Igor had something in his voice and Efina couldn't hear it, she let the chunks go unnoticed. You have to pay attention to a dog. Olaf has a hard, dry voice and besides he doesn't say anything. He barks very little, swallows the chunks in his voice and keeps them in his stomach. He rolls them round in his intestine. He deposes them on the pavement and Efina wraps them in a little bag that she immediately throws into the dustbin. Olaf trots along before her, his thorax tied tightly round his pack of heart and organs. His flanks are hollow because Olaf eats well and gets enough exercise. When she goes out with Olaf, Efina thinks of Raúl. Efina these past months hasn't paid much attention to Raúl. He came out of his bubble. He has stepped to the side and Efina sees him from farther and farther away. His hair is thinning at the temples. His gestures are slightly less round but it might be the distance blurring the sharpness of her vision. The corners of his mouth turn imperceptibly less upward but his smiles are as beautiful as ever although he imperceptibly tries a little less hard when he makes love. Yes, he does it a bit more mechanically but there's nothing to complain about, there still is the right amount of caresses, gentleness, tenderness and roughness. Where precisely on her body did Raúl's hands let go. Raúl from afar looks more like an immigrant. Careful not to lose Raúl in the crowd of men with dark skin, dark eyes, dark hair and eyebrows. Men who have a wife and a dog.

Olaf has an almost unnerving way of always at the same time of day hatching turds of the same size and weight. Igor was a little wild but Olaf is a metronome. Igor on certain days didn't make, or released things in the most incongruous places. It wasn't convenient, really, but there was that imponderable in her life. Olaf's coat doesn't grow, not one hair sticks out though they never take him to the groomer. Igor ran with his ears to the wind and in fact that's what caused his death. But Olaf, what do they know about Olaf. His outings are rigorously measured. His days carefully calibrated. He goes from the basket to the leash and from the leash to the basket. His only moments of creativity come when he's encouraged to play with his plastic bone. But the flat is not big and Olaf is often scolded when he wakes up the neighbours. There were complaints and Olaf made an appointment and came back with his nails filed down at the request of the floor below. That dog, you never know what he's like, because he's always on a leash. Raúl also agrees that he needs to play round freely in the park. There is a grassy circle in the middle where no bad driver or car has ever been seen. Raúl and Efina watch Olaf preparing to take a run in the park. He noses about right next to their feet. He noses about right and left. He hasn't even realized he's completely free. He turns his head towards his masters. His leash invisible today. Today it does not pull his neck. He remains seated, he looks round. Run Olaf, shout Efina and Raúl, but Olaf has stopped sniffing round. He doesn't understand why they're not taking him for a walk, why they're not taking him over there, he senses there are females with interesting rumps over there, but he can't go there, with these two remaining motionless.

Efina is disappointed and she's afraid she doesn't like Olaf. She likes crazy little dogs that jump over hedges. She likes dogs that know how to make themselves scarce. Igor didn't jump, of course. Igor didn't do anything at all, but you could feel he was impatiently pulling on the leash, he would pull away suddenly, he'd circle round strollers, old ladies, the translucent legs of old ladies that had to be carefully disentangled. But Olaf, nothing. Olaf goes straight from point A to point B. He raises his leg at an angle of forty-five to forty-three degrees, the pressure of his stream is constant. Olaf's stream stops suddenly. A strong stream, then nothing more. Igor used to let two or three more drops fall as he walked, because Igor was the carefree type, but Olaf ends cleanly, you have no fear of getting urine on your hands when you pet Olaf's coat. He's a hygienic dog. He doesn't have pus in the corner of his eyes and doesn't give off embarrassing farts. He eats his dry dog food neatly and nothing gets caught between his canines. Olaf knows how to yawn discreetly without breathing the smell of decay into your nose. Only his tongue perhaps can be a bit audacious. Olaf has a wandering tongue, it bears the stamp of Olaf's personality, but no one is perfect in this world. Yes, Efina tells herself, Raúl was really right: Igor was a person, she can see it retrospectively. If she could, she would go to his grave and put a flower on it. But Igor is not buried, he's in ashes in a bag, eliminated God knows how. If there were a dog like Igor again, life would regain its savour. She asks Raúl if he would agree, if they lost Olaf, to get an Igor instead.

Raúl is surprised by what Efina says. It's true that Olaf is not Igor. The difference is obvious and Raúl himself must admit he often thought of Igor while he was taking Olaf out. Strange how Olaf's body, his little thoracic cage round his tightly knotted pack, his hard turds constantly evoke for Raúl the roundness and joy of Igor. Igor that wild, nutty dog. That dope. Igor that silly idiot. Igor sometimes brings tears to Raúl's eyes and he wipes them away at the same time that he's throwing away Olaf's droppings. It's not that he's reluctant to pick them up. But he's weary of making the same gestures every morning. Tear off the green bag. Wrap up Olaf's present. Throw the whole thing in the dustbin. And this, always at the same spot, the pavement in front of the bakery. If only Olaf could move his business forward by thirty or even twenty inches. But no, Olaf relieves himself at the exact same spot and people on their way to work look at Raúl picking it up every morning. Not that Raúl is embarrassed. It's only natural to do this, since Raúl loves

Olaf. But there are certain things one prefers to do discreetly. There is the private sphere and the public sphere. Olaf makes no distinctions. He displays himself on the street. All you'd have to do is move Olaf forward every week by thirty inches and in seven years he could lay his turd on the lawn at the entrance to the park. Raúl could throw the turd directly into the dustbin. Whereas now he has to walk two hundred yards with that bag in his hand. The bag the pedestrians waiting for the green light watch, to see where Raúl puts it as it goes by every morning. Raúl cannot mechanically drop it at the foot of a plane tree or on the curb of the pavement. He is obliged to walk forward with the two ounces dangling from his raised arm until he goes by the park entrance, stands in front of the dustbin and drops it in with a precise gesture visible from the red lights, the cars, the windows and the balconies. How many pounds coming from Olaf did that dustbin hold, ever since Olaf has existed and lived with Efina and Raúl. Luckily Raúl isn't good at maths and Efina forgot, she no longer knows how to calculate how much time it takes bathtubs to empty out. Bathtubs fill up from one side in these maths problems while the stopper is unplugged. Dogs also fill up and from the other end they empty out. A dog fills up, he empties out, it's a law of nature and you take the dog out every morning. Every morning and every evening you take out the dog.

Efina and Raúl no longer eat croissants because of Olaf. Igor relieved himself in the park and they could go into the bakery on the way. Tie Igor to the tree and buy two croissants. But you can't buy two croissants with the bag full of Olaf's two ounces. No, Raúl thinks that's just impossible. Raúl and Efina no longer eat croissants. Igor's intestines were either longer or more patient. Olaf has to lay down his turd five minutes after exiting the flat. The bakery is too far away. Even supposing you ran, Olaf would have to be tied to the tree and Olaf would relieve himself while Raúl buys the croissants and once out of the bakery what do you do. Raúl can't pick up Olaf's turd with the croissants, he needs both hands. He'd have to put the bag of croissants down not far from Olaf's black turd. And who knows what other dogs do at the spot where Raúl would put down the croissants. No, with Olaf, no more croissants. All the more so since on the way back Olaf produces a last turd again at the bakery.

Efina suggested that Raúl leave the bag at the foot of the tree while he buys the croissants, the time for him to go in and out. But Raúl thinks it isn't easy to get rid of the bag: at the lights there are people in the morning, and what would happen if those people saw Raúl put down the two ounces day in day out at the foot of the tree and walk into the bakery. These people are the same every day and when the light turns green, they would never see Raúl picking up the dog's bag. They might think Raúl doesn't want to walk two hundred yards to go to the dustbin and that makes Raúl uneasy. Raúl's skin is dark and a foreigner must do all he can to avoid being noticed. Carry the bags two hundred yards. Raise his arm over the dustbin. Not eat croissants if the dog has relieved himself. Raúl could write a dissertation on the influence of dog turd on the consumption of croissants, but he doesn't have time to write, he has to work, walk dogs. And Efina doesn't have time to write her own dissertation on the influence of dogs' intestines on marital moods either. Efina has to dream, she has no time to write. Dream who knows what, something she wouldn't like to say. She has to dream.

IT'S SUMMER AND THE NEWS EXPLODES like a thunderclap: T is getting married to an actress. Up to now, Efina never attached any importance to T's women. They were there, like the pimples on his skin, like the hair on his head and legs. But this one is a different story. It's passion. Efina can feel it, Efina can smell it, Efina reads it between the lines in the paper where it says that the great actor, T, is getting married. To L, the magnificent actress. The magnificent actress Léona, whom Efina does not like to see on stage. Nor in the movies. Nor in the pages of the newspapers where they write she's getting married with great pomp, and in the cathedral no less, with three hundred guests and a number of stars from show business. T must have lost his mind. He must have gone through a profound change to go along with this masquerade. Or else Efina no longer knows who he is.

T is happy. He has met a woman who is transforming his life into a volcano and who's tough enough to shake him up, and in love enough to make him forgive her cutting remarks. She's beautiful too, so much so that T is helpless before her blue eyes beneath her carefully plucked brows. Violet, Léona corrects him. T leaves her the rudder, she's the one who chooses the flat and decorates it up to the ceiling. Nights with his new wife are like games of chance. T waits for them and dreads them. You never know what's coming: is she going to take the reins and lead him to the point of asphyxiation or, on the contrary, inert and ironic, comment on his performance. Is she going to bite his cheek and leave love bites on his neck a few hours before the premiere or cuddle up to him and whisper inanities in his ear. With Léona, any game is permitted and for the first time in many rotations, T no longer thinks he's bored. He's attractive again. His wife knows how to make him look great, she throws out his whole wardrobe and at T's expense brings in a professional makeover man who reveals the attractive fifty-something inside. With a salt-and-pepper mane. With a little stubble. With chic but relaxed jackets. And renovated sex-appeal of which women—more and more of them—become intuitively aware. T's professional life is improving. He gets many parts and has finally accepted a role in a film. The leading role, for Léona wouldn't have stood for it if her husband was in small letters on the poster. T had vowed on all that is sacred that the cinema would never get him. He had spit on celluloid and lost many of his friends who had let themselves be sucked up by the machine. But he was persuaded. His wife is wiser. Don't be old hat. Films touch people. The cinema is an art. An art made of intensity. An art made of intuition, a far greater intuition than the theatre where actors have all their time to rehearse their lines. But film actors: one clap, and you must be excellent. One clap and you must be someone else. One clap and you have to propel yourself into a world that exists only in a script. Léona compares the actors to world-class sprinters. And which has the most prestige: sprinting or long-distance running. What drains more emotion: sprinters or marathon runners. Who are called the gods of the stadium. No, Léona thinks the cinema is an art a thousand times nobler. Next to it the theatre is poor. The theatre has a shabby side to it. Stuff that costs peanuts. Sets made out of boxes. Cinderella-like costumes. But films, billions. She prefers the cinema. She's not good in the theatre, because her adrenaline doesn't start flowing. She gets her kicks from the camera. When she hears the word action, she has a thrill of pleasure. Léona says T has to change. He has to be in the cinema. The cinema is asking for T and T must become a star. It would be selfish to save his talent for a few measly stages. T should think of being immortal. T should think of having his face engraved. T should think above all of his debts and his children.

T's film career takes off splendidly. He's playing Lawrence of Arabia in his best years. The shoot is to last three months. In his trailer in the desert, T is bored stiff. The cameramen and technicians are absorbed in incomprehensible details. Where are the other actors. They're asleep or they're playing poker. They compare what they were paid in the past and make plans about their future fees which should increase by ten per cent a year. In his trailer, T is bored. He's read all his books. He has a pen. Paper. From the desert, melancholy messages take their flight.

Dear Efina, he writes, I know you're not expecting me and as for me, I think I have nothing to say to you. I have nothing to tell you, nothing to confess and nothing to communicate to you. I'm parked in the desert with nothingness before my eyes. You may want to know exactly what I see in front of me. A scrap of sheet metal. Grey, you guessed it. A water pipe more thirsty than its owner. A shred of brown blanket. A basin where my ankles are soaking. My red, swollen ankles. They are cooking me in a white-hot trailer. I never set foot outside. Besides, there's nothing outside. I can't bear sand and I'm going crazy in this emptiness. I am a frail man, you know. The only thing that keeps me alive is the footbaths my wife has volunteered to administer three to five times a day. How she manages to get the water at the right temperature I have no idea. The fact is that the water is nice and cool and, for a moment, I feel I'm coming back to life. How she managed to follow me here too and keep me company, I have no idea either. And yet the budget is tight, everything has been calculated down to the last teabag, the least square inch they grant us in these trailers, everything is calculated and stipulated in the contracts they whip out at the slightest complaint. Efina, here's a piece of advice for you: if one day someone should offer to enrol you in a film, think it over a hundred times. Don't rush as I know you do, don't charge in head first, take your time and don't be afraid of saying no. It's a word that is absolutely legitimate and you'll see the world won't collapse for all of that. Besides, I don't know why on earth I'm thinking about that, for you know as well as I do that you are not an actress, you do not have that talent and, thank God, life has kept you away from the stage. We both know genius has not been distributed equitably between the two of us. I will grant you this, though: you do have a talent for adding bitterness to life. You give a certain taste to life. You certainly know how to complicate things, so following you is exhausting, but you're pleasant enough, so that one gets caught up in your game. A woman knows how to give. And the one I'm living with and who is my wife, you know that, the woman I married in church and who will surely bury me, and it's all I want and you can be just as sure of it, Efina, even if this is hard for you and even if it hurts and even if you can't believe it, this woman, I know this with certainty: if she weren't with me, in this desert, in life, I now would be no more than a wreck or who knows, already pushing the daisies. This to say how things stand and explain why I share her life and why she governs mine. Someone just knocked on my door. I can see the director's feet through the cracks. I know those feet well. Those feet are clearer in my mind than his face. That man has the toes of a phoney. He buys me by bowing and scraping and does what he wants with me. The sand is making me go limp. I'll leave you now Efina, I can't spend my time entertaining you, you should try to find an interest and a goal besides me in life. I'll leave you hoping that you've become a little more sensible.

Live well, have fun, life goes away quickly you know and in the end leaves only particles floating in the wind. The toes in front of the door are getting impatient, greetings and all respect to you. From his desert, feet in the water and the rest in a furnace, T.

WITH HIS WIFE, T IS HAPPY. This new life satisfies him. He is blossoming and his heart is expanding out for miles. Surely that must be why he writes those love letters. Yes that's why. He's filled with so much love that he feels the need to spill some of the surplus downwards. Down to those who don't have any. Those who suffer and wander blindly. Those for whom the sun is in the clouds. The unhappy. The lost. Those who are confused. Efina.

Efina is choked with rage when she recognizes T's writing on the envelopes. She tears them open anyway and reads the letters at one go. The dustbin is already opening its mouth wide but she changes her mind and puts them away with the others in the boxes. It would be a pity to spoil such a complete collection. Something could be done with it. A show someday. A sociological study. A textbook for medical students. A graphological analysis. The envelopes keep falling into her letterbox. Efina just by seeing them can imagine what they contain. Burning phrases, promises and confessions, condescending sentences. She knows all that, but she reads on:

Efina, Forgive me for pursuing you once more, one more time. There are not many people to whom one can say certain things and given what has happened or not between us and given that special bond that has been flickering for years, I felt you'd be the only person who could read me. Take it as a compliment. I see very little of you but when all is said and done, I think of you as an old friend. Strangely close to me. Strangely distant too, but that's not what I'm writing about. I'm sorry if I'm boring you, and throw out my letter if you think it's dumb. I have to pour out my words. Yes, allow me to open my heart to you and tell you how precious my joy is. Waking up in the morning and seeing my wife on the pillow is for me the purest and most beautiful picture there is. What happiness is mine. And to think I could have missed knowing this person. She is radiant, superb and intelligent, far more than you and I. She's way up there compared to us, and, what's even better, she's incredibly talented. If I weren't afraid of being vulgar, I would tell you about our nights and how exquisite it all is. I often say to myself in the morning that this woman in another life was one of those priestesses of love that may have existed in other civilizations. But don't let all that worry and depress you. Above all, don't get hurt by making comparisons. You are of a totally different kind of course and to be otherwise you cannot. So live in your own way and follow your own character. For the lioness lives like lionesses and the swallow like swallows. In all friendship, Efina, despite the richness of his happiness, you see, your old friend has not forgotten you, T.

Efina, I have all I desire and really life has been too good to me. I have never been so happy and I need to let you know: with no other woman have I been so happy. Still, I think from time to time about the little lark you are and I wonder if you'll ever be able to know such felicity. Undoubtedly, we are not equal and each human being experiences things to the extent he can. Some receive much, others little. We all have a measure of love according to our own capacities. Efina, don't worry if your life seems dull and less radiant than what I'm saying. It's natural since I chose to shine in the footlights while you spend yours hopping round like a sparrow. I say this without being judgemental, for our duty in life is to fill up our notebooks. Mine is overflowing with joy and I would love to give you a little bit of it. The woman who shares my life is an exceptional human being. Our souls—this is rare—are united on the seven levels. I look indulgently upon affairs that had seemed passions to me. They were only little waves. I now know what a body is. Now I know where the soul is housed and I know what the union of two bodies and two souls means. But I don't want to expand on it. Speaking to you of those things pre-supposes certain basic notions and I'm not sure you really know what I'm talking about. Continue to love, exercise your heart. Do not leave it inactive. One day perhaps it will receive what I am trying to describe. Do not hesitate to answer and to send me your prose. Although it is simple, it always gives me something to think about. May your life open out, and with all best wishes, warmly, T.

Efina, I am burning with such passion that I need to see and touch my wife almost two hundred times a day. She doesn't understand and gets annoyed, so the only recourse I have is to write and keep writing. Allow me to send you these few breathless lines. If only you knew how I love her. I'm ready to do anything just to touch her little finger. Breathe in her lioness hair. Get a glimpse of her beautiful eyes. The day before yesterday I took a plane to take a look at her on a set. I had to fly back right away but seeing her again gave me the strength to be without her for another day and a half. She should be here in a little while and so I'm writing to you as I wait. She was divine on that set. She was making a film overseas. For my wife, you know, is invited all over the world. My wife is in demand everywhere. In every country on this planet. But above all in our bedroom. I lit candles. I drew a hot bath and strewed it with petals. I bought her ten presents. A Lebanese caterer delivered food. I'm expecting her any minute now. Efina you can't put your hand on me, luckily because you might send me to see a doctor. My heart is beating at three hundred an hour. Fortunately I don't have a heart condition, for living next to a woman like this, my organ would have exploded. I got ready to welcome her and carefully took a shower. I plucked my hair here and there and sprayed my perfume. I've shaved twice since this morning. I put on a new jacket. Do you think I look good in this jacket. I hope so, it cost me a fortune. Since you're a woman, even though you have different tastes, do you think she'll like it. It's blue, and underneath I'm wearing a black shirt. I don't know if I should button it at the second or third button. Some say no, others yes. The champagne is already in the cooler. The roses will be delivered shortly. Ah I can hear the florist setting down his bouquets at the door. I also thought I heard the door of a car. The taxi is probably downstairs. My divine lady is probably very near. Thanks for your company. I must leave you now. I'll post this letter tomorrow so you can share these small crumbs of joy. In a hurry, but all yours, T. Postscript: A word before posting: that was last night as I was saying and even a thousand times stronger. Thank you for still reading me, T.

Efina, How is it possible to vibrate for such a long time. My heart swells with gratitude and raises me to heights where words seem empty and thoughts almost mystical. Happiness is complete. Mutual understanding, fusion, pleasure, love, all this is too much for a man. For a man and a woman, I should write, so amazingly do Léona and I make one. Allow me to make you the witness of this love which, you must admit, is rare. Forgive me if I only write to you briefly today. I'm afraid you'll be frightened by the violence of what I'm feeling. I wouldn't want to make you envious either. If I could share, you may be sure I would give you a little of what I am savouring. May you know passion. May you, oh yes, have a taste of it. I'll get back to you soon perhaps, Efina. Don't resent me if I remain silent, but now I feel I am entering places where it becomes difficult to write words, whatever they may be. For ever your friend, T.

This is really too much and Efina wastes no time in answering: Dear Sir, she writes, I thank you for having shared these crumbs of felicity with me. True, I have not seen any such crumbs in a long time. I live with my feet firmly planted on the ground. I kiss my husband every day and I don't need to write letter after letter to do so. That you should feel the need to do so set me thinking. Were you perhaps afraid that this spectacle might escape me. Do you need an audience to reach nirvana. You have lived on the stage. You should finally learn to come off it and be able to appreciate life for what it is. Once again you're completely wrong about me. I am happy, but I'm sorry, I had forgotten to write and proclaim it from the rooftops. I'll let you go back to your hugs and kisses. You must know that I do not consider myself your friend or your confidante. At most as an outlet and a box in which to dump your words. Below you will find an address where you can post the pages you keep covering with black ink. It's an agency specialized in comforting lonely hearts. I have just one more thing to say to you: don't write to me. I am happy and sticking my nose into your misery does not make me feel particularly good. My best wishes for the future. Goodbye for ever, Efina.

EFINA IS GOING OUT WITH ALBERTO. Actually it's not official. Efina is married to Raúl but, from time to time, she goes out with Alberto. Alberto is a name Efina has given him out of a taste for secrecy. But in fact Alberto is not such a nice name. She rebaptizes him Alfonso and Alfonso says he doesn't give a damn. He couldn't care less and he doesn't have her taste for secrecy. He's young and serious. He doesn't quite fit the picture of the passionate lover. Alfonso doesn't get easily excited. He's tall, not very muscular. His torso is covered with long, skinny hairs combed like grass at the edge of a

stream. He does a little bike-riding. He makes dates
with Efina at the end of the day in a fancy cafe. He
talks to her about what he's reading. Luckily little
chocolates are served with the coffee and Efina has
cups of it until they can lie down. In his studio
apartment, Alfonso shows her two or three more
books, then Efina kisses him. He takes advantage of
this to quote a certain philosopher and Efina puts
her hand on his trousers. That makes Alfonso think
of a film and Efina strokes his back. He's thinking
of a book again, does Efina know it, but no, Efina
has not read this book and Alfonso is surprised,
really, how come Efina hasn't read this book. Efina
is distracted and finds no answer. Alfonso lets himself go a bit and says that it feels really good, carnal
love with her is satisfying. After they've made love,
Alfonso talks about his old relationships. Not so
old, some of them only date from a few months
back. Efina isn't hurt, all that is unimportant. Those
cute little ghosts have no weight. She listens, she's
faced with an enigma. She knows those girls exist,
she has seen pictures of them, but it's as if those
other women were not real. What happens in bed,
what her Alfonso or her Raúl give her and what she
provides them with, too, oh, how can she put it.

Efina wonders what other women can possibly give. Because, as for her, she's sure she has inside her the three hundred per cent of what makes a woman. Of what is called feminine. What do men find in other women. What do other women give to those men. Efina has everything in her and it is hard to imagine that the women she sees going by in the street are as completely filled with it.

When she gets back home, Efina is sure to find Raúl on the couch. Raúl doesn't ask about her afternoon, the past is of no interest and his eyes are limpid. He has no suspicious thoughts. He hears what is said to him. His back is straight as a stick and his body like his mind goes in one direction only. He has no problem with his weight. He does not undergo torture when he sees sweets. He does not dig into the peanuts. He easily forgets his drink. Raúl is calm and well balanced. For example, Efina is sure Raúl never read the letters. She would have distrusted any other man and would have hidden the boxes, but from Raúl there's nothing to fear and the boxes can lie round the way they are, half open under the bed. She just mentioned that it was old correspondence that Efina was thinking of throwing out and that's all right with him. This husband is all of one piece. You look into him all the way to the bottom and the bottom isn't very far down, Raúl supposes it's the same for everyone. He doesn't have much imagination, maybe that's the detail Efina would like to correct if she had the chance. He has no curiosity and, actually, that's something else she'd like to modify. Raúl is happy with syllables dipped in a bath of just about anything. He's ready to swallow anything you make up. When you tell him you don't know, you can't remember, you're going out to eat with a girlfriend. You're exhausted and you want to turn out the light and sleep, he swallows it all in a white-toothed smile. Raúl omits what's not going well and is always surprised that the horizon can be darkened with storms that are not yet on the road. He looks straight in front of him and if it's sunny, he's happy. If the sky is dark, Raúl goes into a brief hibernation, his eyes are blind, he's deaf. Rarely have husband and wife diverged so much. How could Raúl discover what is asleep below, way down there, at the bottom, eight thousand yards beneath Efina's smiles and face. Raúl does not see the colour of the stagnant water all the way down there and Efina is forced to show him the kind of face he likes to see. Whereas her T immediately plunged both hands into it and when they looked at each other, they stirred that dishwater up.

EFINA WEARS A CROWN OF DAISIES like a girl of seventeen. Her belly is supple and elastic. Her hair long and shining. She laughs and no wrinkle marks the corners of her eyes. Her forehead is smoothed out like a veil. Efina is in love and her fiancé is twenty. He possesses Efina in the bedroom. The act is energetic and pure. A raw bar of energy. Assured, precise gestures reach their goal in a natural way. Pleasure envelops the two lovers at the exact same time. The two of them are one sex and one body. The lovers are finally united. Efina wakes up and the sun is emerging from limbo. She's forty-six and she is sleeping in T's bed. At her side, the imprecise body of her man. The birds are singing, going wild. The birds sing joy joy joy even when things aren't going well, when nothing's right, the birds are tireless and sing at 5 a.m. Wherever she may wake up in the city, there's always a bird to teach Efina something. Efina every morning takes her class in carefreeness. She's forty-seven, she sleeps in T's bed.

Raúl . . . she can't even think about him any more, her chest becomes too constricted when she has to think of Raúl. When she has to think of Olaf. And Olaf and Raúl at the same time, she thinks she's going to suffocate. She suffocates in the morning next to T. The birds teach her a lesson. Joy joy joy. Then T wakes up and the contraction disappears, the great flight forward overwhelms her, T's lips turn into rags, T's body becomes a floor-mop and with one stroke of his tongue he wipes out all the thoughts and worries that have darkened Efina's mind. For that reason, T and Efina need many kisses and hugs to forget. To forget that Léona. That Raúl. That Olaf. That Léona Raúl and Olaf. Olaf Raúl and Léona. If only those three could marry one another. God, what a relief it would be. But they don't even want to meet. They don't even know what they're missing. Olaf is a nice boy. Raúl is a worthy man. Léona is emotionally disturbed, but Raúl is an accommodating man.

Efina would like to go on a trip. Efina and T are staying at a seaside resort, Spelunca, in a grotto that costs them an arm and a leg. Through the entrance to the specially converted grotto, the sea has the blueness of Léona. The spotless walls have been whitewashed. Then they stay a few weeks in a chalet in the Alps. Efina bathes in the mountain streams. Another week in Venice. They travel on the Trans-Siberian Express. They spend a few days in New York. They eat at the Tour d'Argent. They are seen on the Great Wall of China and in the Forbidden City. Efina would also like them to travel to the moon, but T says enough, he doesn't like to travel and, besides, he's not sure they could have afforded all those things. Efina has too much imagination and T doesn't dare say so, he would like her not to think and be as simple as her dog. Efina has a little dog. She missed her Olaf and T wanted her to get a dog. He didn't say that it was also so she would be less tiresome and leave him in peace instead of dragging him into pavement cafes, restaurants, stores, fitting rooms, cinemas, parks and God knows where on this earth. T needs solitude. He does not need distractions. He's not a great talker, he detests conversation. He does hold forth, yes, often, when he's with people and when he feels he can amuse the audience, he launches into stories, he has to impress the table, but once he's home he's mute. He says nothing to his women. To Efina he does not talk. He buys her a little dog.

Buying a dog for Efina was a whole adventure. At first she didn't want to. She didn't want to have one of those cute little dogs. She wanted a dog like Igor, the kind you can't carry in your arm and eats up his two cans a day. Then one day T brings in Tulpi. She's pathetic, says Efina, who from this moment on, has to watch where she's walking. She has to say in her defence that Tulpi's brain is no bigger than the brain of a fish. Tulpi doesn't think of running away when she sees legs suddenly looming over her and what has to happen happens: Tulpi under Efina's foot. Of course Tulpi isn't dead, but still, she is damaged and Efina wishes for a dog you can see and doesn't sneak round under your feet. They don't know what to do with Tulpi, who solves the problem all by herself by having a heart attack during the fireworks. Her ashes are not preserved and T looks for another dog. This time he goes to the kennel. He doesn't want a thoroughbred. He wants a mutt, one of those obedient animals, good-humoured, who don't ask to be taken out and know how to keep out of sight. A dog is not a potted

plant, as the employee who presents several specimens to T points out. A russet dog, affectionate, but
who slobbers. A dog who is frightening to behold.
A pregnant female. A German shepherd. A sausage.
A curly one. A dog with bangs. A darkie. A Chinese.
Puck. Puck has a spotted coat, engaging looks and
the employee swears he doesn't eat much meat. He
doesn't make messes. He doesn't misbehave, as far
as the employee can judge, for there's a lot of work
here and they're only two of them to clean up. But
Puck, the employee insists, Puck is no problem.
Puck follows the flow and never complains. Of
course sometimes he may have let himself be influ-
enced by the others, because Puck loves a little fun,
but Puck is no ringleader and if there's no one to get
him off the straight and narrow Puck stays in his
place like a good dog. He doesn't even like to bark
very much, he's not even much of a joker or dishonest or nutty or anything, he never acts up. Puck
might finally be a kind of ideal dog, the employee
says while T writes his name on the form. And now
that will make an empty cage to clean up. And Puck
goes off, loudly booed by the kennel.

Puck feels comfortable in the house, Efina and T's home. There were a few problems the month he moved in, he had lost his bearings, but now it's fine and Puck can keep it in until he gets out onto the street. The animal behaviourist said Puck is a sensitive dog, a dog you have to treat with caution, but a dog who could give great joy. Efina says he's certainly hiding it well, with his clumsy look and his legs going out every which way when he starts off. Puck is nice, but they're not asking for the moon and anyway intelligence is not what you look for in a dog. You have to focus on the heart and that's something you can find in abundance in this dog. A faithful, loving heart. A devoted, pure heart and boundless affection. A heart that expresses itself through the tongue: Puck never stops licking, he licks Efina on her face, he licks Efina on her feet, so much so that she ends up wearing sleeves so as not to be licked by her dog. But to have to wear a woollen cap, no, that's going too far and Puck is sent to the behaviourist for a few more sessions. Who says Puck is normal. Puck is hypersensitive. Puck is emotional as well as sentimental. The dog must be spared strong emotions and be permitted to lick, or Puck would be disoriented and might fall into a fairly serious depression. Between two evils, choose the lesser, the behaviourist advises, and Efina asks T to let himself be licked, too. It isn't fair that she should be the only one to endure it, she has the right to breathe too. He's Efina's dog, replies T. Yes, but T's the one who bought him, T chose him at the kennel. Did T not see that Puck is a licker. No, T didn't see Puck lick. And perhaps Puck at the kennel was unable to lick for years and that's why he's catching up now. T has no intention of being licked. T is an artist, an intellectual, he does not want to lower himself and it is out of the question that he be licked by a dog. He can accept sharing his bedroom. He can accept sharing his bed. He can accept finding hairs on his jacket and trousers. All that he does for her, not for Puck. He can accept many things. He has raised children. He knows what it means to live a gypsy life or a life of discomfort. He has lived in all sorts of environments. He's not afraid of being bumped round. He lived in a trailer. It's not that he's bourgeois but he will not let himself be licked.

They buy a doll for Puck. He keeps it between his two paws and he licks Efina a little less. It's too bad that Puck should be that way, because otherwise he'd be an ideal dog. He only relieves himself once.

He eats just a little bit of meat. And yet he's strong as a bear. He doesn't bark much, but he barks well and Efina thinks he can fool burglars if they should come. He likes to go out, but to stay home, too. He enjoys watching TV. He loves Efina but he loves T too and it's impossible to know which of them he prefers. He wags his tail the same way for each of them. He's happy to see them and that's pleasant too. Puck is a dog who's always happy and his tail is tireless. One tiny thing bothers Efina nonetheless, it's that Puck isn't exactly white. After three groomings, his coat is still black and grey. Puck's tongue and his grey colour. Aside from that, he'd be the ideal dog.

EFINA AND T IN A BED. No, Efina and T on a bed. Efina takes T's body. She kisses him. T kneads Efina's shoulder blades, sighing as he does so. The sighs become groans and T moans while Efina bites him, strokes him, sucks him and lavishes all sorts of signs of affection on him. T is leaning on his elbow. His broad, fat hand, moist as rising dough, covers Efina's face. A precise, stubborn tongue searches round in the hollow of his palm. T's palm is salty.

124

Efina's tongue is stubborn, it keeps going, as if
water would well up from it. That little tickling
worm awakes in T's back, in his kidneys and guts,
thrusts which throw Efina onto her belly. A heavy
sack drops down on her back. A wet mouth spills
out against her cheek words that couldn't be said
publicly. A mass introduces itself between her legs
and carves out a space for itself. The space is warm
and cozy. T's hand wanders round the area. Efina
expresses her delight. Sounds form in her throat and
also coos, like a female pigeon, says T panting on
her back. He finds a little hole where he can stick
his index finger and his dove is in seventh heaven.
His Columbine is rising on a magic carpet.

EFINA HAS CHANGED. HER BREASTS are heavy and
her waist has become a bit thicker. Her waist is a little less flexible and she makes stops in front of mir-
rors often. It's incomprehensible. Her waist used to
be very flexible. She could bend forward, backward,
move her waist in circles, it was elastic and Efina
had no trouble touching the tip of her toes with
her fingers. She was supple. She was slim. What
on earth could have happened. Efina didn't see it

coming. She's become more rigid. Not very, says T who hasn't noticed anything, but can you trust men, they don't even see their own rolls of fat. When she leans over, she has two thin rolls of fat on her belly. That shouldn't have happened either. She's sure that these rolls, a year ago let's say, were not there. She takes clothes out of the cupboard and tries them on one by one. And yet her clothes fit her, she can get into her slacks and her skirts only feel a little tight at the waist. Yes, but a long time ago, her skirts didn't squeeze her belly at all, they were even a little big. She's sure she has become less flexible. T says no. T is in bed reading a magazine. T says Efina is supple enough in bed and perfect and not wider at all. No no no no. But T doesn't feel like repeating that all night either, he'd like to read his magazine. Efina tries on an old bra. Strange, it is not too small. She wore it when her son was a baby. And yet she's sure her chest is heavier. From T no sound comes. T will never give his opinion on that matter any more as long as he lives. About her chest being heavy or less heavy. As long as T lives, he will not make another sound about heavy or flexible chests. He wants to finish his magazine. Efina thinks he's retreating because he doesn't want to hurt her, about her chest. These big breasts under her sweater. No doubt about it, her chest is heavy. An old woman's chest.

T TAKES WALKS WITH AN OLD WOMAN and a dog. He doesn't seem to like the dog despite his best efforts. He can't manage to say its name and he simply says the dog. Yet the dog's name is Puck. When T goes out for walks, he looks as if he's carrying the weight of the world on his back. Instead of admiring the greenery, he walks with his eyes on the ground and even drags his feet and if this is pointed out to him, he slows down still more. He's not a good walker. As soon as he sees a bench, he walks over to it and sprawls out and the walk is definitively suspended. He's impervious to advice about the benefits of walking, the direct effect of walks on the reduction of waistlines and the virtues of oxygen. On the contrary, he claims walking is not necessarily good for you. There is too much pollution in the city and considering the shape of his feet, the angle of his knees, the configuration of his pelvis, the stacking of his vertebrae and the bumps on his skull, his doctor has positively advised him against it. T is the prince of insincerity. He can spend the afternoon on a bench and claim they went walking. Can say they got plenty of fresh air when they were actually sitting in a cafe the whole time. He can't put one foot in front of the other. A stretch of grass terrifies him. A forest gives him cold sweat. A hill throws him into a dark mood and brings out all kinds of colds, sore throats, ear infections and nauseas for which he has to be evacuated. Yet you'll never hear that T doesn't like walking. T never has deficiencies. This man has no faults. He's not adverse to walks. It's not true that he can't move. That his muscles have become soft. That his muscles, let's be honest, no longer exist. That his body is a carcass in a trench coat. No, T says that he and his companion walk enormously every Sunday and the old lady who is his companion avoids saying in front of people that it's not true and T is a cripple. T must not lose face. He must pamper his image, even if reality doesn't correspond to it. When Sunday comes and she proposes a walk, with the leash in her hand and a slobbering dog licking the walls, T expresses a joyful, enthusiastic yes. He seems to be in fine form for undertaking that big hike, over two miles long, the one they've been talking about for months. Except that once he's out, there's a danger of a shower. Or his shoes hurt. Or he hears thunder. Or he's losing a filling. Or it's too hot. Or he's been stung by some insect. Or he meets a pal, the one he hasn't seen since high school and suggests they go for a cup of coffee. Or he has a better idea. Or his shoelaces tear. Or his sciatica is acting up again. Or he gets bird droppings on his head and has to go wash himself right away. Or the dog gets him angry. Or he has a fight with his companion. Or he feels like a cuddle and the urge is irresistible. Or someone calls him on the phone and it's important. Or he wants to buy himself some gum and you have to go all over town to find a place that's open. Or he's very hungry, or very thirsty. Or he has indigestion. Or a sudden attack of diarrhoea. Or he wants to go see a play and the show starts in half an hour. So T and his old companion decide that this Sunday it would be wiser to take a walk in the park. Besides, the dog will be happy. Puck the dog loves this park. There are trees sprayed many times by Puck and the dogs that come to the park every day. Puck needs his familiar landmarks, it's important, for otherwise he might fall into a fairly serious depression, and between two evils, choose the lesser. T heads for the park, where there's a pavement cafe. The old woman who accompanies him trudges along, alone, with her dog, while T from his chair waves to them and asks the waiter for the newspaper.

T ONE EVENING AT THE THEATRE with Efina. During the show, T vies with a politician for the favours of the woman sitting between them. The politician has beautiful blue eyes in his vapid face. But T has a good paw, soft and heavy. Oh, the woman keeps moving her knee away, but that's OK, T doesn't lack hope and experience. She's the woman of forty-eight and a half that T has lusted after for ages. Speed is of the essence now, otherwise she'll be definitively overripe and her eyes will never have shone in his bed. She's beautiful, this one. Blue eyes. Wrinkles don't mar her face, they make a charming showcase for it. It's common knowledge that the woman is one of the beauties of the town. T tracks her through the crowd to the champagne bar. It's no easy job to track down a woman with another one on your arm, but you can use the crowd, which quite unfortunately takes your companion suddenly away from you. You can bump into a competitor and greet him with exclamations loud enough to make glasses vibrate and heads turn, especially a blonde head whose blue eyes are going to be sucked in. Blue eyes sucked in for one second, but one second is three thousand times sufficient and T knows what is hiding behind those annoyed looks of women dive back into champagne glasses, and those mouths that hasten to throw out some nonsense to the person they're with. The message gets through, T's eyes hit the target and those sucked-in eyes will come back and look into his. That's how it goes and T does not despair of cornering the woman of forty-eight-plus someday. He marks time in the crowd. Efina hangs on to his arm. T sends her off to get some champagne and during this time he makes his way to the other side. Once again he greets politicians noisily so that Efina, who is naturally shy, does not dare approach for the moment. He slips into a circle of ladies and surprises them by taking two of them on each side in his Herculean arms. The embarrassed ladies giggle and T can feel Efina's little eyes in his back. Efina dressed him in a jacket, a white shirt, and T is shining at his brightest. She washed his hair and his well-shaven cheeks make a shiny pedestal for his eyes. His eyes, ferreting and sly. His eyes see that the forty-eight-year-old woman is right near him and he takes her away from her politician, ignoring the anger seething in his eyes. What do you know, here is my very dear friend, exclaims T, and, taking the crowd as his witness, proclaims their old, indestructible friendship. The lovely prisoner is furious. The crowd jealous and admiring. T's arm goes fraternally round the woman's slight body, even pawing her hips. Ah there you are, says the little voice of Efina. T introduces the beautiful woman to Efina. My great, my charming friend. The friend thus suddenly baptized shakes Efina's hand. I'm going to get some champagne, T announces, for we need one more glass. He throws his body into the crowd. Efina and the woman have nothing to say to each other and Efina offers her the glass intended for T. The vacuum must be filled somehow and they ask each other perfunctory questions. Their heads frequently turn in the direction where T vanished. He's been harpooned by some so-called friend and will never come back, even if they perish of thirst or hunger. Ah, how are you, exclaims T, turning all heads towards him. The vague friend is with a woman; she is tiny and charming. T is talking nonstop for the husband, but the repeated squeezes of his hand on the small woman's arm are extremely meaningful. It kneads and strokes at the same time. The woman lights up with all her teeth. Too easy, says T to himself and takes his quest further on. Everyone must see and appreciate him. He was not on stage this evening. Let them see him in the foyer so he can at least perform his own little skit. He talks, he laughs, he's with everyone. Some light flirting with the girls behind the bar who have full cheeks and may not be quite sixteen and have probably never encountered the big bad T yet. Heavy flirting with the woman who directs the theatre, who is a good friend of course, since T has held her in his arms, and the director like the others would surely like to be undressed again but T has a lot on his plate. Detour round an actor who was on stage this evening, well no, you can't very well avoid him and T launches into a long speech about politics, the weather and renewable energy. This guy can wait a hundred years, won't get his little piece of sugar. A group of politicians. Oh, T loves those guys, there are always plenty of them at premieres, they're a good audience and sometimes have pretty wives. T has them eating out of his hand right away, he has mastered their syntax to perfection. Good to see you here, he cries to the elected officials who take him into their circle. T always looks really good in a circle of elected officials. Of course he says whatever comes into his head and isn't afraid of coming up with outrageous remarks which evaporate into short silences. He certainly is completely uninhibited. He's unpredictable and capable of exploding into your chin, suddenly calling you a bunch of idiots, or smacking a very focused kiss on your wife. But T is a riot, he's entertaining, and to have T in your circle shows you're close to artists and ordinary people alike. The politicians glare at T balefully. Their hands hold back slaps. They see in T a flatterer, a boor, an opportunist. When are we getting married you and me, shouts T as he hugs an old woman to his breast, the mother of a magistrate. But Efina's silhouette is drawing near, let's slip out and move further on. Here comes a girl. T winks at her in a way that takes him back to when he was fourteen. The girl blushes and turns away, but T, holding forth all the while, manages to get back into her field of vision. All this, while chatting with women. All this, while chatting with politicians who're sucking up to him as he talks. They're thinking of T for the Prize. His name comes up now and then every year, it's not a done deal yet, they have to get a few more votes. In fact, with a career like his, it is truly unfortunate that T has not received the Prize yet. If anyone deserves it, it's certainly him. T modestly lowers his eyes. At this point, he doesn't know what to say. Yes, it would be good to get the Prize. But. Does he really deserve it. Does he really measure up. Is he a great enough artist. That he won't say and he smiles to the ladies bunched round him. Ladies are a sound investment. They always hold out their arms to you or anything you can lean on. They offer you their eyes, a firm spot to cross the ford to the other side. Efina is now right next to him. Introduce her to these gentlemen, my companion. Stuff her into the hands of these people and by some pirouette that makes them burst out laughing, escape like the king of hearts disappearing up a sleeve. One of the actors of tonight's show. Hi, says T who never could stand this man. The man is young, nice-looking and he has talent, but that's not something T wants to see. He's not afraid of T and has never been impressed by his manners. You were in the audience, the actor observes. Well I had to, says T, pointing to Efina, who is grappling with the politicians. An empty space, then the actor: I'm going to get a drink. Yes go ahead, answers T, scurrying away. He wanders for a little while between the tables. Those grannies dipping their teabags in their cups. Make sure they don't grab you, you might not be able to get up again. T's glance floats over the heads. He has no equal for fleeing people he has no desire to see. Their good evenings bump into his wall, he's not afraid of being impolite.

Here come those two little actresses who were in tonight's performance. Up close they don't look so great. From his third row, T would have sworn that those two were beauties. He would have signed a marriage contract without blinking. No matter how well he knows the stage, he always gets taken in. The magic box, with its three sides. The box that turns ugly girls into beauties. The machine to compress time, matter and space. These two girls are not magnificent but they were jewels within that box. T compliments them. He is of course not talking to the women. He's talking to the jewels of the stage. He puts his hands on their shoulders and drags them off to the bar. Here are my two little princesses, he explains off the top of his head to

Efina (who happened to be in his path) to ward off any reprimand. The princesses are gentle and nice, Efina does not protest. She does not understand what gets into T to make him chase women. T senses that Efina is bored. He gives her a hug but his eyes, out of sheer habit, are prospecting over her head. The actresses are called Annick and Sonia. T prefers their stage names. They are quite ordinary-looking and their hair doesn't look that good. Their clothes either. As far as T can tell in this crowd, they're wearing hideous coats and of course no high-heeled shoes. Astorine and Mélisette! he exclaims, cutting them off. Astorine and Mélisette smile, they're quite used to this kind of mastodon. Here comes the forty-eight-plus woman again. This time the politician has her firmly in tow, she no longer grants T her eyes. Too bad. T leads Efina to the door. You tire yourself out too much, Efina says to him on the bed as she rubs his ankles.

E AND T ARE LOOKING AT EACH OTHER face to face and they are dropping the last shreds. E says T is

selfish. T says maybe, but E is not exactly an angel
either. E says she has no need for a grandfather. T
says in that case why did she pick an old man. E says
that without her T wouldn't survive. T says, we'll
see about that. T says she looks hysterical. E says T
is horrible. At this point, E loses it and lines up all
kinds of terms which seem to have been picked out
of a dictionary. It is staggering to hear the number
of synonyms E has retained in her head without saying them. T didn't know E was hiding a dictionary
in her head. She doesn't limit herself to two words,
her insults have the floweriness, the variety, the polish, the quality of the finest theatrical language. T
notices the flabby skin on which her sunken eyes are
resting. Her clothes. Her ears. Her body that, well,
doesn't give much, and he can't keep himself from
saying it. E is liquefied, a mass of red and white liquid flowing nonstop onto the ground, a continual
flow, a spontaneous cascade, flowing and regener-
ating itself. It is beautiful and terrifying like an
apparition, T can no longer resist mentioning the
Blessed Virgin, and the cascade turns into a cat with
claws, it's incredible what can happen in a hallway,
T says to himself as he looks for shelter. The wildcat
is against him, its claws are extremely determined,

but it's the eyes mostly that catch your attention, enormous, round, red, bloodshot eyes, as story-books say. T thinks of a book from his childhood, that story in the jungle. The wildcat isn't as bristling now and it is rearranging its clothes. What's happening. It seems there has just been a domestic quarrel. Efina was in the hallway with T and at one point things got out of hand and T is no longer in the bedroom. He's not in the living room either nor in the bathroom. He's not locked in the bathroom. Efina used to take pride in saying that with her T never but never ran away. Never. He wasn't happy with all the other ones, but with her, he was happy. And T would say he was happy and would never run away. Absolutely never. No. Running away had disappeared from his vocabulary.

THE PROBLEM IN T'S LIFE ISN'T DOGS. Nor women. And yet in T's life there was always a problem with a woman somewhere. Even when he was in the cradle, he must have had a problem with his nanny. Or with the baby girl sharing the cradle with him. No, this time T's problem is success. If T had to say what his problem was, it would be more with men.

Young men of course, not old dodderers. Men with blue, not salt-and-pepper stubble. With shirts half-open on skin that is not ruddy. Men who do not have bear-like fur on their back and chest. Who don't have a super-intelligent forehead because its border has retreated. Who don't have a specific instrument for hairs in the nose and ears. Who don't expectorate at night. Who have clear phlegm, not acid reflux from the oesophagus. Who don't have a bulging gut. Who haven't given up. Their scalp does not make a fog descend onto their shoulders. Their fingers, pudgy or not, are not covered with grey down. Their knees do not have a tendency to spread apart and remain bent, and so they don't walk like cavemen. In short, young men between the age of seventeen and forty-nine, those young men are ruining T's life. They are too handsome in the theatre and directors like them too much. People like them too much.

As long as T was great and famous, great, celebrated and adulated, it was easy for him to say he didn't care about success and that, for actors, success was just a moment of masturbation. What counted was acting. What was primordial was theatre and once the rite was accomplished, it didn't matter if people laughed, got angry, left, clapped or went crazy. The autographs didn't matter. The bouquets of flowers and the cards slipped in between the petals. Since they were there. Since T had all that. Journalists. Radios. Critics. Photos. Pimply directors who dreamt of having him for their premieres. Great German directors who had their assistants call him to find out if T would be free four seasons down the road. All right, T is exaggerating a little, maybe he didn't experience all that exactly in that way, but he felt the wind of fame blowing through his hair. He recalls the emotion of the usherettes when they saw him come in and the whispering in the theatre foyers. The eagerness of directors to greet him and take both his hands, if they were free of course, and not on the phone or with their mistresses. But the theatre foyer is empty and the usherettes no longer give him an ovation as he walks by. They have become little girls. They look at him distrustfully and wonder aloud if he's part of the production. That's the way it is, things only last so long and T has reached the end of his destiny. The young men are right behind him. They are pushing and they shine on the stage and T is being pushed forward, waving his arms in the air.

He begins to do something he never did before: visiting theatres outside rehearsal time. He comes two, three hours beforehand, he gets someone to open up for him and sits down in any row at all. A director, a stage manager or a woman who turns on lights—it doesn't matter whose hands they are— sometimes turns on a lamp, but that's not what T is looking for. T likes to sit in the dark, the atmosphere of theatres is vast even if the halls themselves are small, and there the mind can wander without bumping into the walls. What does T think about when he's dreaming away in a theatre seat. He loves the absolute silence. He is absorbed in himself. Then from offstage come steps, ladies' or men's shoes, muffled voices that approach from behind the panels and come out suddenly onto the stage. T has noticed that any bad, unattractive novice takes on the look of a tragic heroine when she's standing on a stage. Even without spotlights. Even without a set or a script. Even without a costume, she's enlarged at least one and a half times. She enters, she's standing on the stage. She's badly dressed and her jeans make her buttocks bulge. She's wearing sport shoes, why are women always so dumb. She hasn't washed her hair and it hangs down in strands like noodles.

142

She comes out on stage casually, with her little handbag on her arm. She doesn't know where to put it, stage left, stage right, she hesitates, joking all the while with a voice behind her. She laughs and babbles away. Her babble resonates like pearls. T knows her laugh is inexpressive but it chimes out like the laugh of Shakespeare's witches. Then other actors enter. They're wearing jeans and T on their faces sees limits and bounds. But their gestures take on thickness and soak in the art of the stage. T follows their improvised acting. He watches them come and go, talk, laugh, until the director comes in to put them into their characters. Then T has to hoist himself onto the stage and take up his role as a little terrier.

T loses himself in the silence of theatres. There is one theatre which is red. He likes a theatre to be black. A black cube. A black stage. He does not like gilding. A theatre should be black right and left and up and down. Like the inside of a mouth, or a heart. T once touched a real heart on stage. It was during one of the periods when he had run away again. During the time he was still living with Efina and had started disappearing again. T was sitting in the dark before rehearsal. An actress had come out on stage. A tall actress, dried-out like an old hen. Or like a flame, depending on the way you looked at her. T knew her by sight. An actress who could have become famous but who'd spent her life just on the verge of success. Always somewhere on the poster. Always with critical esteem but public indifference. And yet she'd hung on and performed regularly. She had preserved, along with her wrinkles, a delicate neck, long arms and vaporous black hair which she dyed once a week. An old woman and a young one at the same time. T had seen her enter on stage. Thinking that she was alone, she had checked the arrangement of her blouse by raising her skirt very high. T is not a voyeur and he coughed discreetly. The actress had been slightly frightened, but an actress knows how to control herself and in a voice that didn't shake at all she called out: Who's there. T walked forward, she was happy to see him and they exchanged a few pleasantries at the director's expense. Directors normally have their cast rehearse in various rooms before playing in the theatre, but that one was particularly presumptuous and wanted to see his actors on stage immediately. T and the woman had a few more

laughs at the expense of the director and T told a
few more stories about previous productions, then
the actress asked T why he was in the theatre an
hour before rehearsal. T didn't know what to say
and the actress said she always came early. Especially the first time. Despite years of experience she
needed to take her time, take the pulse of the theatre.
T nodded. They exchanged a few more nasty stories at the director's expense and then T, short of
material, told a few more that he'd heard someone
tell but about another director—already dead, in
fact. Silence had settled in. And as T had felt the
emotion of the actress, moved to see him so near,
the old instinct returned and with it the old gesture
of the hand going down the neck, stroking its down
with the thick part of the thumb and the other hand
apparently hugging her waist tenderly but actually
making sure of its grip on the prey. The old gesture
of the mouth leaning forward and plastering its lips
on hers and the tongue entering inside, not to taste
its sweetness but to make sure the victim was con-
senting. After that everything always goes quickly
and T's fingers found themselves in the old actress'
skirts. She then straightened out her skirt, ashamed
and happy, and T had pretended to be stirred, but

145

inside him he thought he should cut off his hand and slice his wrist with an axe if that hand now began to rummage through skirts without preliminary consultation. T had felt pity for the actress, that's why he'd taken her in his arms and felt her head trembling against his chest. He had breathed in the suint in her vaporous hair, squeezed her shoulder blades and when he'd judged enough time had passed, he pulled away from the actress without looking her in the eye. The actress passed a hand over her brow, which was white and rather smooth, ran her hand through her hair and said she didn't know what was happening. T had to hold her against him again and cradle her like a child to avoid facing her and he heard himself murmur words which made him very much afraid that the old actress would become infatuated with him. The old actress was indeed infatuated and she confessed things which were rather embarrassing, like a thirty-year attraction and the certainty of a shared life. T had hugged the actress harder and his voice seemed to slip between blocks of stone while he confessed that other woman at home, that Efina in his life, and he had gently closed the gash opened with this actress, put everything back in, healed it over and sewn it back up. The actress had thanked him and T felt ashamed because he hadn't given her anything. With lowered eyes, she said she was just an old hen anyway and T had to take her in his arms again. He looked at the time behind the actress' back and saw it was urgent to conclude so as not to find himself face to face with the rest of the cast. He said some consoling words. His nose in the vaporous hair and his mouth up against her ear, he said now it's as if nothing had happened. They were only partners now, like old pals. And as the actress remained glued to him, T added that she was beautiful, tremendously beautiful, drop-dead beautiful, beautiful as a flame and not like an old hen, like the queen of all the women in Egypt, and the actress had agreed to unglue herself and show him a smile. A weak little smile. Luckily, because the actors had arrived and the rehearsal had started. T's life is full of those wounds that can only be closed with big pushes from the hands and feet.

T AND EFINA LOSE SIGHT of each other in the stupidest way possible. T runs away one Tuesday morning, as he often does. Efina doesn't call him on his cell, contrary to what she usually does. She's fed up with playing the anxious wife and she knows that in any case T only answers one time out of ten. One time out of fifteen or a hundred. T forgets his phone in the park. In the theatre. In a taxi. He gives it to a vagabond who seemed likeable because there was a kind of spark in his wrinkles. He forgets it in a coat and the phone is ringing in the cupboard. He drops it into rivers over every parapet. T owns cellphones in several riverbeds. Efina traditionally gives T a phone for his birthday, at Christmas and from time to time as a surprise in the course of the year. But T must be deaf as a bat or the ringtone isn't set well. He never hears it when it rings. Besides T can't possibly think all the time about turning it off or on. Or about recharging it. He gets a telephone and then when the battery goes dead, the phone stays on top of the chest of drawers for months. T says he no longer remembers how you listen to messages and all Efina's messages are chattering away somewhere in space. What is strange is that Efina has sometimes seen him use the cell, texting with great dexterity. So T runs away that Tuesday and Efina thinks he's going to come back and there's no point looking for him. No point sending messages into orbit crying into empty space. Efina is not a tragic actress. She has her own life after all.

T sleeps in a hotel. He wanders from park to park and from bar to bar. He drinks tea and the waitresses think he's in a detox programme. They're nice to this gentleman. He looks pensive, he always seems absorbed in his thoughts. They'd almost take him under their wing. It's because of the trench coat. A man with salt-and-pepper hair, slumping posture and untamed hair in his nose should not walk around in a trench coat. Or he'll be taken for a vagabond. Especially if the trench coat is stained, a bit torn, and if from its pockets things keep falling on the floor at the slightest gesture. For example, a writing pad, a pen. For in his hotel room, T out of boredom writes often. Always that old habit. He cannot find himself between faded walls and set his eyes on a plywood table, his toes cannot make contact with a rough, suspicious-looking wall-to-wall carpet without feeling a surge of desire to throw himself on the bed and write page after page. He does not know to whom these letters are addressed. What is certain is that they are not for her. No, precisely, not for her. He tells himself he had a thousand of them and she counted no more than any other woman. Yes, none of them is more important than the others and that's exactly what she doesn't understand. They are the set through which he moves, a landscape in which he carves out his life and has to mould to make it comfortable. To give it the thickness and softness of a good mattress so T could lounge on it as on a bed of ease. Fall on it with arms and legs spread out as if on a layer of fresh snow. But snow is made of crystals and science says they're all different, as numerous as they may be. Ever since the creation of the world and the dawn of time, there has never been a snow crystal exactly like another and T's job is endlessly to keep on picking them up. It would be foolish to turn away the ones that come into his hands. When he grows attached to them, he feels that his body is dense, while the crystals float around, immaterial. There is a deficit on the scale and it is perhaps for this reason that T piles them up and keeps receiving them, so that the two pans of the scale should balanced. Efina does not know she's being weighed on one side of a scale, or she thinks she's sitting on it alone. Whereas she shares the scale with a hundred thousand women at the very least. Efina thinks she's the one and only and that's why she tires herself out running after her T with repeated phone calls. A whale net would work better. She thinks T warms powerful feelings for her in his heart. She thinks he has never loved and before her, his affairs were only arses and butts. Butts, arses and tits. Mouths, vaginas and thighs, but hearts, absolutely not: T's heart has supposedly remained virginal and immaculate for Efina alone.

All that is T's fault for respecting the good old basic commandments: Thou shalt not pour out your heart and thou shalt not ostentatiously display thy former love affairs. Thou shalt not talk women to women. All experience thou shalt deny and thou shalt live with a woman as if she were the first. Thou shalt bury inside your heart all trace of old feelings and erase first names. Thy slate shall always remain black and thou shalt not keep pictures in thy wallet. Thus T pretended that he never had any love affairs. That his heart has remained intact and sealed. Efina is the first woman he has loved and the only one who ever owned the key to his heart. Actually, T has been going through hell ever since elementary school, has fallen in love and had affairs that tore him to pieces. T's heart has suffered so much, has been pierced by so many spears, knives and needles that it resembles a piece of meat ripped apart by wild animals. A heart particularly vulnerable and tender but no one besides T knows that. No one besides T and his countless girlfriends who discovered in the great man the heart of an inadequately weaned calf. A heart that easily sheds big tears and, in spite of everything, falls for every girl it meets, to tell the truth. A heart that bleeds for itself but on which it would be dangerous to rely. A heart that takes to the hills as soon as the alarm sounds. Efina did not have the time to fully assess that heart, T stole off just before she could do so, and besides, with age, he has learnt to dissimulate better.

Efina tells herself that, after all, T knows where his home is and always ends up finding his way back to the fold. She goes about her business. A week goes by, goes by quickly. T thinks Efina no longer cares about him because she no longer makes those calls that have the knack of exasperating him. Yes, but at least before that, he knew Efina was thinking about him. Whereas now this silence, the silence of hotel rooms and plywood nightstands, of warped landscapes on the walls and Van Gogh reproductions, unhooked shower curtains, toilets down the hall, sullen night watchmen—this silence is worse than telephones. Another week goes by, less quickly. Efina does not call and T does not come back to her.

He has walked by from time to time. Not too far from her house, he walked by, under the windows, and he did not dare raise his eyes. Another time he did dare but he had the impression that Efina was having some people over. He doesn't know why exactly. Perhaps the light in the living room. Perhaps the window open in the kitchen, a sign that Efina had done the cooking, something she doesn't do very often. In fact, never. Except when Efina has people over. But she never has people over. At least when T is living with her. So Efina is leading a different life and T no longer dares return.

A third week has gone by and Efina doesn't know what to do. T left, it's up to him to come forward. To say: Can I come back. To make amends. To be found one day on the landing, sad and crestfallen because his keys are no longer in his pocket. Three weeks went by without a sign and it's almost too much to suddenly call T. To suddenly say: Where have you been. Your post is on the table. Or so-and-so called. And incidentally: I miss you. And does she really miss T. Efina is sad when she thinks of him. On the other hand, there are some advantages. The wash takes her less time. The bedroom is always neat. She's no longer perpetually awakened during the night, she no longer has to listen to the story of his nightmares or distract him from his insomnias. She no longer has to protect the dog and stand up for him against T. She can call people. Yes, there are some advantages. Yet there is a void, but is that void really big. Efina is beginning to doubt it. She managed to spend three weeks alone and she doesn't feel so bad. Hardly a few tears from time to time and a few rushes of anger. She takes Puck out every evening and morning. Puck watches TV with her. On Sundays, there is also Puck, and all her friends who have returned as if they had been held back for a long time by a dam. Efina thinks she has to wait, it's not up to her to decide. If T comes back, she'll welcome him with joy. If he does not come back—she can't imagine that. Never to see T again. To see him only on the stage. To run into him one day on the street and simply say hello. To kiss T like any other acquaintance.

T is in a fix, too. He has waited too long to go back and if Efina had no problem letting three weeks go by, that means she doesn't want to see him any more and she's turned the T page once and for all. Or perhaps she's angry. But for now T prefers to stay underground, as Efina's rages are cataracts and it's better not to linger beneath them. Two more weeks at the hotel go by and T is beginning to get used to it. He has his bench in the park and sniffing animals go straight by it. He has his chair in the cafe and the waitresses bring him his herb tea and the drunks don't think of bothering him any more. He has his bed in the hotel where the cleaning lady puts on fresh sheets in the morning and lets him flirt with her. He's welcome at the theatre and at the unemployment office. The woman in charge took pity on him and assigned a lady to him who could sort out his papers. T spent some time with her, one thing led to another and he found himself in her bed. Not in the hotel bed, in the lady's clean white bed. T identified her as a potential hostess. She attends to his every need. She's a very good cook and her food is light, her dishes suit his stomach, not like Efina's meals which give him acid reflux. She is calm and attentive. Not like his Efina who stirred up the air in the rooms and yelled for three dirty socks. She's discreet and doesn't ask questions. She may not be very pretty but, after all, Efina wasn't so pretty either. Her skin may be wrinkled in certain areas and her age may not be that far from T's, but T is ready to try even the most unimaginable experiments. At least life has toughened her, she does not conjugate the verb to love, she doesn't talk about love. She is serene, she is available, she works—which leaves T with time for daydreaming, she knows how to be unobtrusive, she knows the schedule of his stomach, which means that T never has to wait for a hot meal to materialize before his eyes. She knows how to go to bed and sleep if T is tired. Or go to bed and do acrobatics if he's up to it. She makes chocolate pies. In short, T lingers in her place and he sometimes thinks he should marry her, because she's the ideal woman. He just has a hard time remembering her name. It's only natural, after such an opulent life. One cannot remember everything. One cannot immediately get everything straight. It's only natural to make mistakes. The brain makes its selection, but it keeps everything inside its cellars and it's only natural to say Marlene instead of Cathy, Cathy instead of Sandra, Sandra instead of Julie and God knows what strings of names T's brain will come up with if something is not done about it. Better not to open T's brain. Better to close the lid and even press down on it a little to stop names from escaping. T now says Darling and this woman contents herself with that.

This woman is wise. She knows T has a girlfriend in another house in the city. She knows her name is Efina and she even knows her by sight. She knows T is a wandering tomcat and he'll leave the house if he feels someone wants to catch him. She says she's not counting on him, he's like a holiday boyfriend, she's surprised to find him on her bed in his morning pyjamas with his hand on a writing pad and milk spilt on the sheet. She does the wash without complaining. From time to time she goes out, without him. She tells him about her dinners and T is a bit jealous. But she does not take him with her. No no no no, it is just not done, T must not forget that in this city, it's his fault that a woman is suffering. A woman who did nothing to hurt him. Who gave him shelter, which T has fled without so much as a thought. No. His new companion refuses to take T along out of feminine solidarity and some nights he mopes there dejectedly. She's enjoying herself far from him with other people. For her, he counts for nothing. He would like her to become attached to him and so he prepares surprises for her.

True, surprises à la T, things that don't take any effort and produce the greatest effect, like: his hostess' nightgown spread out erotically on the sheet; a heart drawn with ball-point pen on a handkerchief, or even on toilet paper; on the mirror, a word written with eyeliner or Dior lipstick; a freshly shaved cheek instead of a porcupine; a little kiss on the cheek; a sparkling, nearly white smile that smells of mint for a change.

The new companion receives these signs with a smile. Her complexion is golden. Her hair short and light brown. Her eyes crinkled. A smile is perpetually on her cheeks, even when T turns on the light in the middle of the night because there's the sound of a mosquito. The smile is caught in her wrinkles, it will never get out. Her flat is white. The walls, the floors, immaculate. She stands in front of the window. She smokes a cigarette, her eyes on the wall across the way. Her eyes always crinkled. Forget-me-nots are caught in the folds. It is striking to discover their crystalline wells in the wrinkles. She is toppled onto the bed. Her head at the edge is hanging upside down. T plunges his eyes into the wells. He bites her neck and her arms which are hardly withered. She's reading on the couch. Dark

158

head, wrinkled like a fruit. She's not beautiful when you go over the details, she's beautiful in another way. Beautiful is too precise a term. It is a generic term that only applies rarely, you'd need a unique, specific adjective for each woman, thinks T as he looks at the head on the white cushions. Her tanned body gets out of bed. Thick at the buttocks and hips. Thick at the arms and legs, and you can't say that her breasts are at the peak of their glory. A body smooth as driftwood. Her movements are round and harmonious, so that it's a pleasure to watch that full, smiling, ripe body come and go. That ripe, serene, reassuring body going into the bathroom. Going into the kitchen. Making a sound of doors and cupboards. Bringing coffee in bed. Thinking of bringing cheese. Thinking of bringing baguettes. Thinking of bringing biscuits. T is never hungry but how nice it is to hear a solid, warm, harmonious body concerned about his subsistence.

NO, T's PROBLEM ISN'T WOMEN. Right now, T's problem is definitely the theatre. Theatre, theatre, theatre. For T, there has never been anything in life but the theatre. If he didn't have the theatre, he doesn't know what would have become of him. A road worker perhaps, although he has fragile lungs and can't stand rain. Gigolo wouldn't have been completely utopian, he had the talent. Writer or poet, possible, but he's still lucid enough to know that his prose isn't worth a cent and the critics would have torn him to pieces. No, the theatre was his life and T is relieved he grabbed that chance. To think he could have become an office worker. To think he could have continued that commercial training which suited him like earrings on a dog. Luckily fate had written on its scrolls, engraved in a wax seal, chiselled in stone that the theatre would find T, T would find the theatre and between them a perpetual wedding would be celebrated to the end of time. Or to the grave, in any case. But even in the grave, you can keep playing a part in the theatre and T had made a pact with a friend: the one who remained would go to the other's grave and act out that famous play where one of the protagonists has died. A dead man who is resuscitated at the end. But it's possible to find all kinds of arrangements in the theatre, isn't it, so that the one who had died would have the impression he was acting. And the one who was alive would have the impression that his friend had not passed away.

T no longer knows where this friend lives. They used to see each other and then, without knowing how, they didn't meet any more after who knows what event. Oh yes, it seems that T couldn't stand his uninspired way of acting, his forced tone and his repetitive diction, and perhaps the actor couldn't stand T's criticisms either. Well, some people are very sensitive and T can't be friends with people who can't take the truth. Anyway, T doesn't have any friends. At his death, would that actor come to his grave. The pact was made, whew, maybe more than fifteen years ago. Maybe more than twenty. And if the other one dies, what would T do. He doubts that he would ever go act over a grave. To act on a cross, how dreadful. In any case that actor is alive, T can read his name on programmes and carefully avoids all his plays. It's easy, the guy doesn't act very much any more. Like T, probably reduced to poverty. Theatrical poverty, of course, because the other poverty—the money kind—T doesn't even know it exists. He has no idea how much money he has in his bank account. He doesn't even know if he has one. His women look after those trifles and as to how they pass the baton, that is something T has never thought about. Women take care of money, that's the rule. It must be a thousand years since he's walked into a bank. It must be two thousand years since he's seen a bill. The money that comes into his hands goes from his hands to his pockets and from his pockets into the hands of the people who sell pads and pens. It goes into the hats of the homeless or lands on the desks of the hotels where T rents a room when he can't take it any more. The money from his pockets falls through one hole or another. It sometimes scatters over the pavements. You could make a fairly decent living by following T step by step on his stations of the cross through the city. From parks to cafes and from cafes to theatres. Because, well, yes, he feels he's an object of pity, but it's stronger than his pride—he has to be in the theatre. Even if he doesn't have a part. Even if the technicians look surprised to see him. Even if the director who knows him greets him with embarrassment and his presence makes the actors fall silent with emotion, he must be in the theatre during the day and watch a rehearsal. Or sit in the dark. Or sit in the foyer. Or, if the theatres are closed, sit in the cafe across the street. Mondays are bad days for T. He doesn't care about what they say. He can see very well that people fall silent and begin acting again once he has sat down, somewhere between the sixth and seventh row. He's very much aware that his presence is not welcome and the annoyed looks of the director do not escape him. Especially when T barges in. When he analyses the acting, takes the floor and doesn't give it up for half an hour. But just try to move a theatrical monument like T. Just try to send a man like that packing, someone who carries as much weight as he does in a theatre. To suggest to this man to take, forthwith, a long walk. To shut his trap once and for all. Just try to move away a living legend in his decline, in a trench coat to boot, and you'll see hordes of actors expressing their indignation. Actors rushing to his defence and launching into veritable tirades. Outraged actresses and young ones with one foot still in the conservatory hurling insults at the head of their respected director, threatening to go on strike, raising their fists at the first rows. You'll see ten thousand Antigones suddenly arise and swear they will leave the stage instantly if T is not allowed to stay. If T had to leave the theatre, if he couldn't attend rehearsals. If he had to swallow the innocent little remarks uttered in so timely a manner between the sixth and seventh row. The directors retreat. T holds his sword over their heads.

That's how T strikes the eye of a fashionable director much talked about in the newspapers and on the radio, who didn't remember T. Until he runs into him in a theatre and feels in all his skinny body and the lenses of his eyeglasses what a magnificent performer this great actor is. Great, monstrous. A gorilla. A sea lion. A mammoth. How can one forget the icons who made the theatre what it is. Old stage icons still have a right to act. True, they may be crumbling, but they have been moulded, they have substance, something that took a whole lifetime to form and it would be a pity to discard them. The director is a communist, all for sustainable growth. He approaches T and hires him.

When you hire T, you have to take one or two precautions. Make sure that T had never come into conflict with his future partners is the advice of old directors who weren't born yesterday. And didn't swear he would remain silent when these actors were around. Investigate this and never hire actors who are touchy or disturbed. This is already a hard thing to do and the young director struggles to find actors T has never criticized, never assessed scathingly, never accused of being the death of the theatre, never touched their wives or pirouetted round their daughters. And apropos, second, do not hire actresses with supple thighs. Choose actresses with a tough hide. Do not underestimate T's ability to sow discord among a group of women. Warn the ladies if necessary. If necessary, think of decoys for T by hiring a gorgeous student as a technician. A beautiful blonde for the lighting. For stage manager a pretty brunette, and as stage technicians three graces who know how to keep him hoping. Better T should have a crush on the tech team than on the cast. Third, avoid hiring young male leads who are either arrogant or too handsome. T does not like to stand in anyone's shadow. Fourth, assign T a chauffeur, a nanny, a cook and an assistant. Fifth, find him a studio flat, across the street from the theatre if possible. Sixth, take out a good insurance policy. Seventh, ask T if the script is to his liking and if he doesn't loathe the author. Eighth, forbid him to have a pen. Ninth, put your director's ego in the freezer.

Once all these conditions have been met, it is possible to put T on stage and it's possible that the show may approach the perfection of the heavenly bodies. The play might be indescribably great, with box-office reservations till God knows when. Ink might flow all over the world and journalists pour out of the central station for him. Perhaps even out of the airport. Queues in front of the box office might go three times round the block and you have to hire traffic controllers with the agreement of the municipality. People hoping to get tickets might spend the night in their sleeping bags. You might have to set up a campsite. Block off traffic. Set up a medical tent for the women who pass out. Move into a larger theatre. Cancel the rest of the season. Even if it's exaggerated, that's what you might expect, but as far as they're concerned, the old directors would never, but never, take the risk of hiring such a dinosaur. They could make a list of all the shows that began leaking, if they had the time and not so many things to do. Of all the shows that sank because of T, all the way to the bottom. The number of directors whose career he shattered. You could mention a rope round a certain neck. The number of actors still on anti-depressants. The number of actresses who had a secret abortion, not counting the ones who hid their children under the names of false fathers. The number of tears shed. The number of cries shouted. The number of curses that made eardrums vibrate.

This being said, it's fair to recognize that those eardrums vibrated in the same way at scenes that young people today cannot even imagine. Magnificent images that remain imprinted on countless retinas to this very day. Dozens of children were named after the characters T played on stage, which seemed fine names to bear. Buckets of tears were shed, squeezed out by T's power. Teeth shone in the dark and chests swelled with laughs coming up from the belly. All that by the grace of T. There are brilliant memories: the night when T blew his fee on a hundred roses for all the usherettes. One hundred roses for each actress and one hundred roses for the ladies behind the ticket window. The nights when T would make a speech until 1 a.m. extolling his leading lady after the actors had taken their bows. The year T played that king and would go out sporting the ermine collar. It is a fact that his roles inhabit T, more than the other way round. T in a role is no longer himself. He lives totally under a different name. It is a proven fact that T is unbearable, and prodigious onstage. Knowing that, let the young director weigh the pros and cons. Let him decide according to his intimate conviction. Let him go to a fortune-teller. Play Russian roulette. Let him face up to his responsibilities. Hire T.

T is full of good will. But he couldn't let anyone see how lost he was and how much he missed the stage. He let himself be coaxed a little and at first he put forth a whole battery of reasons as to why he couldn't go back on stage. He has a bad back. And he's not exactly in his prime any more. One must make way for another generation. He has lost interest. But if the director insists and really wants to take the risk of hiring an old nag like him. If he's truly convinced it's not the young leading actors but an old fart like T. If he's sure it's not beauty but really experience he wants for his play. If he wants to be encumbered by an old sausage. Well, T at this point, defeated by such resolve, gives in. He agrees to go back on stage but he's aware that he's lost his flexibility, agility and grace. The director can still change his mind at any time, old T won't be mad, he has one foot in the grave, but as he says these words, his eyes are shining, his foot is setting on the stairs to the stage and his hand is asking for the script, so the director is eager to get on with it. To direct his fat puppet. To put T on the stage and have him perform. To rule the animal with an iron hand and make him come and go, kneel, roar and die. To lead the brute by the tip of his nose. He has chosen a play with five female parts, two small male parts and the title role for T. A schedule has been decided. Rehearsal dates set. First, learn the lines. Second, work in the studio with T. Third, work on stage with T and the other actors.

A second-hand actor has returned to his companion. He learns his lines in the living room. She watches him from the other end of the couch. The text is being constructed inside her walls. In her home, her cushions, her tiled floor and her stairs.

T AND THE DIRECTOR REHEARSING in the studio. One side of the studio is a slanted glass wall with different coloured panes. Some are smooth, others translucent. Some are yellow and rough. The light they filter is interesting. It soon grows hot under these windows and T is acting in a short-sleeved shirt. That allows him to display, for the benefit of the director, his fleece-covered body. His flabby arms. His stomach rolls. His stocky, crimson neck. If someone had told T that he could take pleasure in being admired by a man, he would have rolled under the table with laughter. And yet, what is happening. T moves about with satisfaction under the eyes of the director, who is fascinated by the brute he holds under his whip. Brute in the figurative sense, of course, because one can feel in T—in his arms or hands perhaps, or in his slightly loose neck—something fragile that is breaking and constantly gluing itself back together again. But as far as the rest is concerned, charisma and force, energy and instinctive power, the director has the impression that T's presence can be felt for miles around. His voice makes the glass wall vibrate. His eyes make the hair on your arms stand on end. You really have the impression that the sun followed his gesture as it suddenly comes through the clouds. T's flesh vibrates when he's loved. When he's admired and someone finds him handsome, his talent blossoms, shines, and he becomes capable of the best of the best, if his audience thinks he's good. If they think he's bad, it's not worth talking about, it's a terrible catastrophe and T can't act any more, so he hides this behind sulky moods, tantrums, whims and scenes, until the show goes down the drain. But if he's adored. If he's admired as he is by this little director. If people are captivated by his acting. If all eyes are upon him and importance is given to his slightest blink. If he's taken care of like a luxury item. If he's placed on a pedestal. Then, yes, T, who is neither ungrateful nor stingy but generous with his talent, is capable of acting like a god when the flame of adulation warms his heart.

The young director makes a fuss over T. He pats his neck and knows how to cover his corrections under layers of creams and perfumes. T is living in the golden age. He loves the play. He loves his part. He loves this director and he loves this studio under the roof with its filtering glass wall. The thing that still bothers him is who the other actors might be, especially the women, whose names he doesn't know. The director assures him that all five of them are excellent, the pick of the crop. (Every one of them.) They are, all five of them—and he emphasizes this—very young and could be his daughters. Yes, he insists, those five young women could be his daughters. They're practically just out of school. That doesn't mean a thing for T. He has hardly ever seen his daughter. And as for the two male parts, T doesn't ask too many questions. Contrary to what people say, he doesn't take all the credit for himself. He makes way for talented actors. He never puts down the other men. Unless they're terrible, of course, and unless they're children—he can't stand playing grandfathers.

A RUN-THROUGH AT THE REHEARSAL STUDIO. T and his female counterparts are going to act together today. The two male actors are absent, they have minor roles and enter at the end. They rehearse the first act. For starters, T is fifteen minutes late. Only natural, for a first time. After all, T wasn't going to take the risk of seeming to wait for these young ladies. He took his time, a good margin. He put on his red scarf—a sign that he does want to put himself out, and the flag isn't flying high yet. He walks in and he looks as if he's wearing blinkers. His nose points towards the ground, his head is rigid. He is able to see, however, since he goes straight up to the director, to whom he speaks surprisingly fast. Before getting to work, the director, who still needs to settle something, asks everyone to wait for him for five minutes. T walks round in circles near the glass wall. He does not take off his trench coat, because of his decadent body. It was really stupid not to have taken a walk every day as Efina thought he should. He shouldn't have taken those naps, he would have a nice, flat stomach. He should have dyed his hair, that strikes him as obvious, it's really amazing he never thought of it. That salt-and-pepper hair makes him look like an old cat. He should have changed his clothes. That vest— when was it washed. Luckily, it seems that under his armpits, the odour is not perceptible.

He noticed the brunette. Not bad, considering the actresses they have today. He turns his back on those girls but the air blowing from their area is loaded with lovely promises. Their voices are a hundred per cent feminine. He is standing in front of the glass wall. The panes are frosted and you can't see out. Nonetheless, he stares at the glass wall and so he won't look lost, he whistles between his teeth as if he were in the street. He glances at the girls. No, let it not be said that T one day looked ill at ease. He walks to the middle of the room. His hands are in his pockets, he is totally nonchalant. He walks back and forth humming to himself. He knows the five girls are watching him. His belly and back are shy, a big pool of shyness. His head turns towards the five. His eyes show he's no chicken. His eyes calmly examine. Meeting their ironic stares makes him an even bigger show-off and he sings a little louder, two or three nearly audible stanzas, then hears bits of phrases coming out of his mouth like: So, how's it goin', girls. Let's get down to work. We'll have to roll up our sleeves. No one answers and his partners immediately think he's a stupid boor and take an instant dislike to him.

The director is back. He asks T to make himself comfortable and T takes off the trench coat and sends it flying into a corner of the room. Same for the shirt and the vest. The bull is in the arena, is he going to be ripped apart. A white bull, no one's ever seen that before, in any case, not a phosphorescent one, and the girls exchange looks that need no translation. The rehearsal gets underway. T knows his lines and his inflections by heart. He could let himself go but he detests being interrupted by the director. It is unbearable to be abruptly cut like that. The other days, it all went well. The director used kid gloves, he was all ears for him, all eyes, all body, and he took precautions every time he cut him off. One correction was compensated by at least thirty-six compliments. Whereas now, T is being handled like a piece of furniture, an armchair or a table, he wonders to which of them he is being associated. Modesty and humility in this profession are cardinal virtues and T is the first to say so to anyone who hasn't learnt his lesson. Only, don't tell him that after two weeks of one-on-one rehearsals he still has to be corrected. Don't ask him to change his style completely, when he has grasped the meaning, the essence, the very marrow of this role. He has understood it and ingested it. He has digested it inside his body and inscribed it in the nuclei of his cells. He had discovered such beautiful things that should be displayed and now suddenly they want to throw it all out of the window. You'd think the director was doing it on purpose, telling him off like that, while his partners, who are hardly dazzling—even if they have some talent—are almost never corrected and T is beginning to see red. The director sees the red, because he announces a five-minute break and takes the time to slip something to T, to slip into his ear how brilliant his acting is and how, even though he knows him by now, every time he sees him, he's so impressed. Nonetheless, this is not sufficient, for the director has not taken the precaution of saying this loud enough for the five little geese. T says he's tired and sits on a stool while he watches them work. The director reads T's lines, which is a problem for him, after all, and the actresses call for T to get back into the play. Flattered, T gets back on his feet and the rehearsal resumes.

There is one passage where T plays opposite the brunette. T reprimands her for something and she stands up to him. They're like two roosters ready to peck at each other. Two rooster heads bristling against each other, waiting to be close enough to blind the other with a stab of the beak. To fling their hooked fingers forward and grab everything they can, for example, brown longish hair held back by a ponytail that can easily come unravelled, and a sponge rubber band that can fall in the wink of an eye—and the director steps in. What's happening in this scene all of a sudden. The script does not say that T should tear his partner to pieces or rip out her hair, nor that the actress should start screaming. T apologizes profusely: he doesn't know what got into him, he got carried away by the script and put too much into it. The actress asks for a break, the time for her to straighten her hair and regain her composure. T follows her into the bathroom. Really he didn't mean to. He was probably stirred by her. He probably lost his head because of the boldness and charm that he never expected to find in such a young woman, and so on. Then the little traditional kiss the girl would like to refuse, but can you refuse something so sweet. The problem is, the next scene is a love scene. The director decides to first rehearse the scene where the prostitutes talk about T while T is spying on them. Then the one where T argues about money with his girlfriend. The one where T barges into the living room and thinks of committing suicide.

T gains in assurance as he acts. He's pretty good in every scene. His partners are up to it and generous enough to pass him the ball. At times he forgets to think, he's totally into it. The refreshing rest of acting. Ah, that good vacancy of the brain: it had been a long time since he had taken this flight to his heaven. What a delight, when the body moves without thinking and the mind doesn't throw its grains of sand into the works. Lightness. On a scale, T would weigh zero kilos. He's acting at the very top of the ether. Weightlessness is too heavy a word for it. His subtlety is dazzling and by the end of the scene, he has earned the compliments of the actresses, ill-disposed though they are towards him.

The director is worried. He knows these animals well. He knows that like on a graph, peaks give way to ravines and he advises T to hold himself back just a little. The premiere is a month away. The tank should not be empty when the curtain rises. During rehearsals you have to act at eighty per cent. If not, what will happen during the two months the play runs. T would be emptied to the bottom. T would be completely worn out, that's the way you end up putting holes in yourself and the director has seen plenty who went directly from the stage to the hospital. The sun is beating on the glass wall and everyone goes down to the cafe. T sits at a table on one side, the five actresses on the other. The director hesitates, then sits down with the girls.

THEY REHEARSE AND REHEARSE. T has gotten to know the five girls. For each he has his witty line and he gives them nicknames. Pretty nicknames of course, although there are one or two of them whose face is not that attractive. But they all have

178

under their shirt pairs of X chromosomes. The girls have tamed him. They dare to come up to him and weave flowers into his beard. Figuratively, it goes without saying. They dare to joke with him and tease him, but not too much, you should see how T's eyes fume if he is bothered too much. His head goes into his neck and he knits his eyebrows. His breathing quickens. Beware, T is a man to be handled with care. But T likes their teasing. He's got used to these women. And they're damn good actresses. Really, he would never have believed it. These girls from the new school of acting are just splendid. There is hope for the world. And then it's endearing to see how they take care of him, they think of bringing him drinks and they ask nicely how he feels, if he has slept well. It's not because he's older, no. It's because he has charisma that they fight over who'll be the favourite and sit in his lap. That spot is hard to fill, he would like to have five laps to seat five favourites. Let's say four, as there's one whose features are less harmonious and whose body has failed to bloom gracefully. But T is not superficial. He studies minds too.

ONE DAY OR ANOTHER, THE LOVE SCENES do need to be rehearsed. One day or another, and that day has arrived. That day must arrive somehow, else the evening of the premiere would find the actors completely at sea at the foot of the curtain, their gestures would not have been decided, their movements in space not meticulously blocked. The stage would be a shambles and so would their brains.

The young director got up reluctantly that morning. He knotted his tie. It's strange, normally he doesn't wear one. At breakfast, he nibbles a little. He kisses his wife, traces a cross on his child's forehead as he saw his father and grandfather do, he doesn't know why. He takes a big briefcase with him. Usually he leaves with his hands in his pockets, his papers under his arm, two pencils in his breast pocket. His wife doesn't say anything but she's thinking. The director goes to work. He's going to have them rehearse The Scenes. It's a fine afternoon, there is light in the trees. He buys a pack of chewing gum.

T gets to the studio early. He's in a good mood and astonishingly carefree. Well, it's a bit surprising that T should remain seated on a stool facing the glass wall, a place where you can't see anything, but

180

you always have to avoid asking yourself questions. The race of actors likes to be different. Some wear wigs. Others extravagant dresses. Some shear off their hair or parade round with a cane. Others carve out a bohemian life for themselves. And others sit with their back to the room facing glass walls through which nothing can be seen. That's the way it is and there's nothing you can say about it. That's the race of actors. But he, the director, who only goes on stage to explain a gesture or shake the hand of the stage manager, wears his hair short and no one turns round when he goes by in the street. He has a wife, a child. No one notices him on the bus. He's like everyone else, except now. He opens a door at the side of the theatre. He walks up a few little flights of stairs. He comes out into a room and five pretty girls come out after him like spores. Then he claps his hands and shouts out in a voice that seems to surprise his shoulders: Take your places, everyone.

Today he's going to have them play something tricky. Today he's going to have them rehearse Love, and he doesn't know if it's something sublime or rehashed mush. In his heart of hearts, he wonders if he really has the right CV. He has known three

women and a half in his life and lived through seven
big domestic quarrels. Perhaps that's quite enough.
He never had two mistresses at the same time. He has
never known passion, the flooding of the Mekong,
only unions that flowed quietly by. The separations
were carried out calmly and by mutual agreement.
He never thought he'd die of a broken heart and his
heart has never yet secreted its self-destructive poi-
son. Take your places, everyone. The director
announces the scene they're going to start rehearsing. T acts dumbfounded, a man who thinks the
scene has already been perfected. It is a complex
scene in three stages. T, almost drunk, on the couch,
shares caresses with his wife. The script does not
say what happens. That's the way theatrical scripts
are, there always remains a vacuum here and there
between the words and between two small letters,
there is always some space into which one can slip
an arm or a tongue. Or a finger or a leg. But T is
immediately warned that what's written is written
and allows no room for over-interpretation. But all
that is only the prologue. When they've stopped
cuddling, the wife is to fall asleep while T, sobered
up, hears the owl hooting. It's the signal that his
mistress is now beneath the window. His mistress

182

joins T and they exchange tokens of affection. The
director explains that given the situation, with a
wife on the couch, those tokens of affection can only
be furtive. When they've stopped fondling each
other, there is a brief quarrel between the two about
money. The mistress leaves and T, peeved, finishes
off the bottle on the end table. He then falls asleep
and the three prostitutes of Scene 3 visit him in his
dream and lead him into a bacchanal. At this point,
the director feels he has to tell the girls not to worry,
he'll explain in due time the gestures they'll have to
make and as far as the costumes go, no worry either,
they'll hardly reveal more than a nipple. The girls
tell him they couldn't care less, they'll show their
arses if he wants them to.

So now T is clued in. T declares he's ready to
go. He feels strangely shy. He swaggers about. It's
one thing to play around in a hotel room amid the
noises of plumbing and under the ten eyes of warped
cardboard sunflowers, and another to kiss under the
eyes of a director who checks to see if T's doing it
well and isn't going too far, amid the giggling of
these brazen girls. His wife makes him swear that he
won't use his tongue, even on the evening of the last
performance. If, coming out of his embraces, the

actress rolls her eyes in the direction of the other actresses, it can only be from embarrassment. T brushes away the idea that a woman in his arms could find the situation unpleasant. Anyway, the couch will not remain in the annals of the stage. For his part, T had so much difficulty with those fake caresses that he feared he would be disgusted with them for ever. That mouth had a dry taste. An owl is hooting weakly. Ah, that's a pretty good imitation. That little brunette has talent. Now she hurries to his side. She is sweet and her lips are on fire. She talks to T while looking into his eyes and what takes place resembles the torch of real love. At certain times, T lets himself be taken in and then some literary turn of phrase brings him back to acting. It's a play. Theatre. This girl is not in love. I have never loved you so passionately, says the brunette. I am still the same man, stammers T. Do you still desire me. says the brunette. Yes I love you madly, stammers T. Enough, says the director. Could T articulate. Yes I love you, T articulates. And still more tenderly please, T. Have you never felt these things. Have you never loved in your life. Think of a woman you know. Now let's do it again. Articulate. Yes I love you madly, T articulates tenderly. Ha ha ha go the actresses. You are the man who holds love in his arms, the brunette continues. Here the play mentions a kiss. T pretends not to see it but the director intervenes. He feels the need to explain what's at stake in this scene. Apparently it's important. He explains what's at stake in this kiss. This kiss expands to fill a good quarter of an hour. This kiss takes up thirty minutes and the director concludes by quoting the authors who thought it should be put into the repertoire. To hear him talk, you'd think there was only this one kiss, perpetuated all over the earth. A kiss that began three million years ago and has endured until this very day. Would T mind participating today in this kiss that began with the jaws of two hairy hominids. The director is sorry but he found T mechanical. T should appeal to his senses. Appeal to his memories and recall the women he has loved. Hasn't T loved women teases the director while the women laugh among themselves. If he looked hard, T would have no problem finding in his heart two or three memories, says the director with a butcher's knife. Isn't he a Don Juan. Isn't he a seducer and isn't it true that he has the same long list of conquests they teach in acting schools when it comes to Don Juan.

Yes, the conquests were indeed excellent. And there is indeed a woman. But her image is so fixedly kept in his mind that it would more likely produce a paralysing effect. No matter. It's the prostitutes' turn now. T had often resorted to this kind of expedient and he feels at ease. True, they're never as cheeky and vulgar. All that comes right out of the folklore of the theatre. He ventures to point this out and takes the director to task. Doesn't he think these women men pay are actually never so outrageous. Has he never observed that. Of course, says the director, blushing, things happen in a more ordinary way. But, T insists, has the director also noticed how those women who are so dazzling on the pavement are as ordinary as your own woman in the bedroom, so much so that you forget you're paying them. Correct, says the director, and he asks the actresses to tone it down. Play it like ordinary women. The words will be strong enough to characterize what they are. The words, right. They are rather crude and Mademoiselle Malicia, especially, expresses herself as if she were biting into a piece of meat. That Malicia is clearly the ringleader. She's the one who leads the others and turns the scene into an orgy. An orgy or almost, for here the director insists on saying

that he prefers to suggest things. Not that he's prud-
ish, on the contrary, but he doesn't like it when
everything is shown and he's thinking of having the
stage directions said rather than acted. No problem,
T assures him. He never liked plays where the audience has nothing to do but slump back in their seats.
On the other hand a transparent canvas. On the
other hand, lowered lights, bodies you can't see dis-
tinctly. On the other hand, an object removed from
the stage. These are things that give people more to
look for and in a way attract the audience to the
stage. The director is absolutely of the same opinion.
He decides on a ten-minute break. Rubbing the soap
on his hands, he scrutinizes himself in the bathroom
mirror. This play is absurd—the audience won't be
interested. And T in the middle of those girls. The
director will look ridiculous. He looks at himself
close up. A drudge. A microbe. He's going to go out
and see more women. He has to have affairs. His list
has to get long enough to go beyond his ten fingers
so that when he counts them he'll fall asleep. He
cherishes his wife far too much.

TODAY'S THE DAY OF THE LAST PERFORMANCE. The show is sold out, as it is every evening. Somewhere beyond the curtain sits T's new woman. His new companion there on red velvet, that's interesting. And what about his Efina, is she here. Is there an Efina in the house. Would Madame Efina please go immediately to the dressing rooms. She is wanted in the first dressing room. The dressing room on the boys' side. She's wanted in a dressing room where someone is thinking intensely of her. Thinking about her with irritation, but that's not what's important, she's being thought of and one wonders if a lady of that name is in the house. That lady has to show up, or someone's brain would not function well, someone's body would be clumsy, some actor's mouth could commit blunders that might ruin his aura. Destroy his reputation. Say the name Efina on stage, for example. Stop following the script for example and stammer umm umm. Have that lady come forward. Too late, the actor is wanted on stage. T enters. He steps into the light. He assumes the gestures of his character. The voice and thoughts of a person who does not know an Efina and who has never even heard of a lady with such a name. How restful to find oneself in the bones of a man who has never known that woman. Who has not written letters to her. Who has never been subjected to her dog. Who never carried the rages of any Efina on his back. What a relief to know nothing about that and never to have gone through life with her name on his arms. T is performing like never before. He's taking his flight. He has been touched by grace. His face, overwhelmed with emotion, is streaming, is it sweat, is it tears. The audience is giving him a standing ovation. The old ladies, sucking on their sweets, whisper to one another, it's him, it's T. Young men, gaping, feel vocations being born inside them. Girls fall in love and make wishes, they give their bodies and souls away. Men in their inner selves make amends for the times they appeared weak. They have seen virility. Women blush and rub their thighs. Old folks change their wills. All palms are stinging and the audience is summoning the actors back on stage. Calling T back on stage.

T has come back for a bow. He has a hundred bouquets in his arms. He has ten thousand roses under his feet and he doesn't know what to do. This is really too much. He is submerged by grace. Cry—but that wouldn't be enough. Smile—but that would be inadequate. Thank them—but the audience doesn't care. T motions that he's going to say something. The hindquarters of the audience fit snuggly into the velvet of their seats again. There is a moment of silence; you could hear a fly buzz if there were flies in the theatre. It's strange, there aren't any flies, there are never any mosquitoes. Never any spiders, cockroaches, ants, never any wasps on the stage. T wonders if the directors have them shooed away or if there is a special spray to drive flies away from theatres. No, of course not, they can feel that those men are fakes all by themselves. Flies can smell a fraud. Flies can immediately detect what is not authentic. What is not flesh and blood. Flies are not going to swarm round a Macbeth. They're not going to swarm round a Poupoff. They're not going to waste their time on a Peer Gynt or a Prospero. On a Hector or an Estragon. T's life has been the life of a ghost. He has lived for nothing. A puppet, a figurehead, a wooden marionette. Pinocchio. His life has been spent in the theatre, where insects do not come. Where odours do not exist. Where no corporal humour is exuded for real. Where people don't live for real. Where no tear comes from the heart. Where no laugh comes from the belly. Where kisses are mechanical. Where words are stamps glued on mouths. Where the borders of time are blurry. Space there is contained in four crates or by sheets hanging from ropes. It is not brimming with life but forced and artificial.

He bows before the black hole. Some hands still want to applaud but he waves them to stop. T is now going to speak. He opens his mouth, his eyes diving into the abyss. A row of faces gleams at its edge like a row of teeth. Thank you, T articulates. Thank you. Clapping of hands. Bravos. Thank you. Thank you, T repeats. Clapping of hands. T raises his hand. Tonight, proclaims T the great artist at the top of his art. Tonight, says T with a certain stiffness in his voice. Tonight was the last performance. The words leap out of his throat and jump far from him into the dark. Tonight I would like to say something. Silence from the dark. This last performance is also mine, I will act no more. One huge cry issues from all throats. Loud whistling in the darkness. Tonight I'm through with acting. I dedicate this last performance. Louder whistling. A whistle that doesn't want to stop, ever. T, the audience shouts. I dedicate this last performance. Whistles. I dedicate this last performance to . . . T, shouts

a woman in the audience. To my wife. Silence from
the dark. To my wife Efina . . . Clapping of hands,
storm, downpour. Stamping of feet. Thunderclaps.
The curtain falls. Whistles. Handkerchiefs dab eyes.
Hands do not stop clapping. The curtain rises. The
great actor is no longer on stage. The stage,
immensely flat. The great actor is in his dressing
room, from which never but never in all eternity
will he come out. He will not come out for centuries
and centuries. In the dressing rooms, the bouquets
are waiting. Like every evening, bouquets with a
solid scent, bouquets of funeral lilies. The scent of
the flowers weighs tons and takes up every inch of
space. The assistant conscientiously reads out the
cards she picks between the petals. The cards have
curlicues on them that are resolutely feminine.
From a larger, whiter bouquet, still more fragrant
and thicker, a thick cream-coloured card edged with
gold is extracted. Raised initials make a distin-
guished seal. The assistant unfolds a page and reads
it out. T is sprawled out over a chair. The thing facing him in the mirror—he cannot recognize it. It's
a thing he has never seen. His mind cannot move
forward any more. It has stopped on this chair. It is
suspended in the dressing rooms of the theatre

where he has acted for the last time. It is melting among the bouquets.

The assistant reads: T. Allow me to write to you, in the name of our passion, in the name of our marriage that you buried by running away. The assistant glances at T. He has spilt over his chair. I have been silent until now and stopped calling you back. I did not try to please you or lecture you. I did not want to run after you and I thought you were from that time on, out of reach for me. No, I could not look for you again in that house of yours, the theatre, where you know I am not particularly welcome. The theatre for me is a cube. I went round it many times, the door is closed for me. I cannot distinguish between the windows. No matter, I will be there this evening. I come only to see you and you know how much it costs me. I will be in the audience tonight and my presence will mean that we're tied together, you and I. We have been married. We shared beds. We shared spoons and saliva. A piece of your being is in me and it will remain firmly lodged inside me. I would like to make this bond known and show everyone that talent still unites our two minds. Now you're shining in the theatre and I'm shining on the screen. What was one has been split and is now doubled. Let this bouquet be the expression of what is still blooming and can take shape again between us. Love and kisses for our future, Léona.

The assistant opens another envelope without raising her eyes. She found it in a bouquet bought at the supermarket. T, she reads. We thought it preferable to write to you on one single card so as not to flood your dressing room. We really wanted to salute this last performance. Salute your talent. Repeat to you in writing that you may be a great actor, but you're still a poor lover, a lousy husband and an elusive father. You will find in this little card the memory and homage, the remote and disillusioned greetings of: Your Women United.

Another card comes out of the roses. Dear T, reads the assistant. I am writing to you on a black card. Forgive my irony. Let me simply say that tonight I will welcome you in my bed, whatever may happen on stage. All yours, Your new companion.

Other letters, with no bouquet. The assistant reads: Good luck on this last performance. The Corner Café.

Break a leg tonight, from the sommelier ladies of the Café de l'Union.

The cafe the Wandering French Fry sends greetings to T and wishes him all the best for his show. Congratulations, Eva and Cindy, your waitresses.

Still another bouquet, smaller. The assistant tears open the envelope. T, it says on it. Take this simple bouquet as a sign that I forgive you. I wrote you wagons of letters. Remember only this one, for it will be the last. Your weight in my life has been enormous and phenomenal. I don't know what this weight is or if love is the right word. I'm sure your acting was excellent. There was no evening I was free to come. E.

A small fly comes out of the bouquet and lands on T's forehead. A small worm moves over a leaf. A middle-aged man is crying, his nose in the flowers. The fly pumps up the tears on his forehead.

THE THEATRE IS DESERTED and it's Monday, the day it's closed. The outside is perfectly quiet. Out of the dressing rooms, a grey man comes crawling in a trench coat. His new companion is carrying a bag where theatre people throw the stuff that piles up in dressing rooms from one performance to the next. The bouquets have been left with the caretaker. T has also left behind his stage costume, given to him by the company as an exceptional souvenir. The costume he wore on stage was custom made in an original fabric and cut, it is in the cupboard on its hanger. And that costume in the cupboard, T knows exactly what will happen to it. He can see other actors coming in. Actors for a show with no costumes. No set. No director, practically no actors and most certainly no audience, T consoles himself, sniggering. He can picture them opening the cupboard, complaining that it's not empty, joking about the costume, obviously ridiculous when it's on a hanger. They'll hang their jackets over it. They'll take one costume or another and end up using it on stage for their underfunded play. Some people will recognize the costume and think back to T in his glory days and it will be as if it had been sold in the flea market. Or the actors will throw the costumes into the dustbin and it will all go to the ragpickers, if they still exist. His costumes will be burnt along with the regular rubbish. The company that burns rubbish will realize that something is burning less well than the rest. A man will go down into the vat with a pike and a mask, he'll look round in the garbage and pull the tunic and its golden buttons out of the filth. The canvas trousers. The costume which was strange, not from one era or another. That costume-maker was gifted and she was also very pretty, time was too short, T says to himself as he sprawls over the white cushions.

You think problems go away, you think you can get rid of them. Problems stay with you once and for all, in time they grow heavy and take up more space as old age settles in more comfortably on your lap. On your shoulders, on your hips, on your back and on your head, T complains to his companion who gives him back massages and brings him tubs of water. He's always had the gift of seeing from the inside the effect he has on others. And what can you see now. What can she see, the one with the crinkled eyes, a white flat and a white bed on which T not too often topples her and shows her his virility. The same one suggests sitz baths to him and rubs his joints with ointments advertising: for the relief of old bones. Or: for the relief of osteosenile pains. But T is not a decrepit old fogey. It even seems that, at his age, some men are mature and dashing. Some, at his age, marry sweet young things and the young things don't seem to be complaining. They rub up against them lovingly. He must have got old before his age. It's the stage that demands the sacrifice. Could the theatre devour one's flesh and blood in the end. Could the theatre wear out its own tools. True, you act, you live, time is obliterated, you die on stage many times, you play at putting on white beards, you release silos of emotions, you suffer, and you're surprised at middle age to have aged more than the others. To have more wrinkles on your face. To carry more bags under your eyes and have your back more bent and your belly slightly more prominent. You dig deep into the very marrow of your bones and the marrow has its limits. The marrow is not inexhaustible, inevitably the day comes when you reach the end of the deposit.

T explains this to his companion, who is lying up against him in bed. They are naked and the woman's hand is on T's thigh. On his thigh but no farther. Farther, T would not like it. T would turn on his side and bury his face in the pillow. His shoulder would have to be patted, the little hairs on the nape of his neck would have to be stroked for a long time before T would turn round and show his distressed face. Her hand is on his thigh but it can't go any farther. Farther on, the idea of consistency would inevitably come up. You couldn't help evaluating its degree of tenderness. You would have to judge its softness. Yes inevitably, if you go farther, you won't be able to stop yourself from thinking of thickness and this must be avoided. T and his new companion naked on the bed, chatting. Their eyes wander over the ceiling. The ceiling, or the white walls. Over the white curtains and the white paintings. Over her breasts and robust, brown body. Over her feet and legs. Over her belly, her fleece, which is slightly golden. On T's body too, eyes have the right to wander. Over T's feet, his calves. His arms and hands. But on the middle of the body, careful. On the middle of T's body, eyes would also be obliged to evaluate its tension and this must be avoided. You may look at his toes. You may look at, let's say, his belly, but this is less tolerated. You may even eye his baldness if you're a little kamikaze. The eye may touch his body, but once it reaches a specific spot the glance must be elliptical, otherwise T could be hurt. He could consider himself humiliated. He could pass out and the day would be ruined. If not the week. At any rate, there are certainly enough things to observe. The walls, which are white. The paintings, which are white. The ceiling, which is white. The woman's body, which is brown and warm and lets itself be looked at all over.

WHO IS T WRITING TO DURING THE DAY. He settles into a sitting position on the bed. He puts a cushion against his back and a cushion on his legs. He puts a cup on the pillow and the sheet must be changed often, not merely on wash days. T's companion, who is beginning to be not so new any more and is beginning to resemble the others, this woman wants a dog. She was pleasant. She spoke little. She took care of the house and T liked her silences and her tidy flat. The smoke of her cigarettes which put a screen in front of her. She has stopped smoking and now she's looking for a dog for herself. The music's playing an old tune, T says to himself, looking for a way out. And yet he really liked the woman. He'd even managed to remember her first name, Chrystiane, with a *y*. But there you are, the new companion has given up smoking, she's getting fatter, she wants a dog. The dog is supposed to stop her from getting fat and bring her thigh measurements down to an acceptable figure. T couldn't care less. Thighs can be fat or not and anyway he always thought this woman was rather large. Beauty in this woman is not what interests him. Rather, substance or density, perhaps. He says so and instead of feeling honoured, she begins sulking. Now that's really a first. He's always seen her smiling. But this time, T will have to leave through the door, this time it looks like it's over and for once, the decision comes from the woman. T won't have to run away. With her hand on the doorknob and her smile a bit less broad, she explains to T that she's grown tired. Since T said: me or the dog, the woman, with full knowledge of the facts, chose the dog, because T's not the one who will reduce her waistline down. He's not the one who will care about her health. He's not the one who'll greet her happily and give her signs of affection. T is an old egoist. An old tune, T repeats to himself as he hits the road to the hotels again.

Hotels during this parenthesis have become more sordid. You'd think they took advantage of it to drop a star. Some have been renovated, but they

seem even more visibly dingy with their prefabri-
cated bathrooms than with the good old leaky taps.
Let's see, what would this or that character say. T
always had a good memory. He can recite all his
parts, or just about. His career passes by his eyes
and so he's never bored and time passes. And so you
bring in other voices, you talk constantly, you could
also go mad, but luckily T is a very solid man, contrary to what his women have said from time imme-
morial. T is well balanced. He certainly has to be,
considering the vagaries of his life. Any other man
would have lost his head already, he would already
have screamed out of the window, screamed naked,
and the police would already have parked their van.
He would have already sent off all kinds of anonymous letters. The proof of his sanity is that he sent
nothing. That he could remain for so many days
locked up in a hotel room looking at pink walls and
reciting dialogues. That he didn't send off those
pages which he has an urge to fill. Any other man
but T would go mad but T keeps his sanity. Could
it be because he writes so many pages. Could it be
because he covers whole pads with ink. Perhaps, but
that's not important, since stamps are something he
doesn't buy. He never got envelopes either, he just

fills up writing pads. A man has the right. There's nothing that can prevent him from doing this. A man has the right to fill up pads in a cheap hotel room, the right to leave them lying round and the chambermaids have the right to decipher them, provided they have the time and know how to read, and drop the handle of the vacuum cleaner: Dear Efina, on the pages.

AN ENVELOPE LEAVES THE CAFE. A limp sheath whose edges, however, remain rigid enough to stay in a vertical position. T can't stand drunks any more, he has gone beneath their crust and what he saw is not appealing. Those waitresses with their rugged faces, he doesn't feel like seeing them any more either. They're not funny. His walk is not very steady. He drank his two camomile teas. Returning to his memory are the words he heard at the moment of separations. The fateful phrases of departures, the vade mecums freely given during break-up scenes. Those syllables he never took the trouble to gather in his clasped hands, always turning his back on them instead. Those words stuck to

his shoulder blades without his knowing it and travelled with him. Now they've gone round and fly
back in his face like pages of a newspaper in the
wind. The wind has turned, says T to himself as he
wipes his face to get rid of them.

There was one woman who was extremely
angry, she was yelling with her hands on her hips.
T was contemplating that farm woman at the door
of her cottage and a smile curled the corner of his
lips. The woman's anger had redoubled, her fists
dug into her hips. If T remembers correctly, some
very bad language had been used in front of that
cottage, yes some really heavy words; then the door
had closed and T had been sent packing with a valid
passport for hell in his pocket. In his pocket and on
his coat and perhaps stuck to his skin, and T has
every reason to believe that he will soon reach his
destination. But the path is always longer than you
think and there are always stops along the way. For
instance a stop at that weird skinny creature pierced
by rings and spikes. She's sitting on a bench and her
eyes go right into his. T is surprised, and realizes
she's a woman for him. One of the lowest category
no doubt, but feelings, like mussels, latch on to the
most precarious bases. T's alliance with that young

woman creates a sensation, it makes heads turn on the bus. The girl covered with quills often snuggles up to him, T holds her cautiously. It would be dumb to hurt himself. No one has ever uttered for T such superlative words. No heart has ever been bound by oaths so pure and it's certainly the first time anyone wrote him poems. T is not far from thinking something might be possible when the girl vanishes into thin air, along with his writing pads. Brand-new pads, unfortunately. It would have been better if she had taken the pads already blackened with writing which T intends to throw into the dustbin, even if he never does.

HE IS RECOGNIZED ON THE STREET. The friend doesn't understand why T says, Hello Director. But it is well known that T has become a kind of wandering driveller, a drifting dropout who no longer finds a home to sleep in. Besides, a slight odour is coming from his shirt collar and its rim is rather dubious. T observes the other's face, which rapidly regains its composure. It is deeply wrinkled but the eyes have remained the same. It's the voice which is recognizable. The voice and its inflexions, which transport him onto the stage. Here is the friend of his early years, who shone with him in the theatre. His path ended or rather continued in regions where T never went. The friend pats T on the back, it takes some courage to do that, but friendship must show that it can triumph over repulsion. They sit at a pavement cafe. The fake straw chair hurts T, his overflowing flesh has got into the habit of annexing objects. The ex-friend is of an intelligent species. He has always known how to hold forth, make brilliant analyses and spout on and on for journalists. T too may have given the impression that he was of that kind. They provided animated discussions when they were twenty-two or twenty-five. Back then, T used to carry a pack of cigarettes in his breast pocket, never too far from his lips. Then T became an inflated balloon while the friend travelled through life with his elegant house of cards, of an architecture hitherto unseen. Journalists can catch a glimpse of him through a little window he installed in the front of his head. The ex-friend can direct himself on stage and has more than one string in his bow. He's done some directing. He can write reviews. He even published a slim volume of essays. T's letters next to that would look like the scratches of a screech-owl. He married and probably divorced, at least once or twice, and his marriages must have lasted three times longer than T's. He must have taken care of his children and he surely took them to school in the morning. Does the friend have children, inquires T. The answer is affirmative. Two fingers are shown on his hand. And how many wives. The ex-friend has no desire to stir up mud but he assures him that his experiences have been fruitful and, in life, everything has a meaning and an end too, isn't that right. He smokes his pack in silence. So there too, he has hung on, unlike T who has never followed through with anything and is impossible to pin down.

Watching the ex-friend draws a smile from T. He might have put ashes on his hair and a make-up artist may have drawn bags under his eyes. He might have put on grey make-up and a fake wrinkled brow made of plastic. A fake skull too, why not. And over it, that wig. He may have cushions under his jacket. At this point the ex-friend is going to speak. What he's about to say seems important, his eyes go serious, whereas T is back thirty years, on the topic of fun with women. The ex-friend squeezes his cup, his eyes on his hand. T and he were friends. Great friends. Even if certain things happened and they lost sight of each other, T and he are friends for life. Here the ex-friend raises his eyes to check if T agrees and T, who is as cowardly as a scared cat and could never keep his word about anything, nods in agreement. The friend would like to know if T recalls the vow. The vow, says T to gain a minute. Yes, the vow to act over the grave. The friend in a few words refreshes his memory. One of them was to act over the grave. The grave of the other who would be dead. The friend on T's grave. Or T on the friend's grave. Here both of them involuntarily examine each other to see which one is closer to his demise and which one has more chance of acting on fresh soil. You never know, anything can happen very very fast, says the ex-friend who comes out of the judgement a winner. He does feel in very good shape but health isn't the only thing. There are also accidents. There is bad luck. Fate. There is rotten luck, concedes T, who has no intention, really, of leaving the scene too soon. Life isn't always fun. But to make your last bow just for that, no, there are things you can endure and you have to be ready for all kinds of compromises to survive. Even having crippled arms and legs. Lying in a bed. Reduced to the four walls of a bedroom.

T, as long as he can still breathe, as long as a pen can hold between his index finger and his thumb, and his ears can perceive the blackbirds' songs on summer mornings all tangled together like a piece of steel wool, well, T will consider himself more or less alive and content.

The ex-friend does not share this opinion. He is astounded that a man can simply not care about his arms and legs. He's stupefied that someone can consider himself satisfied, stuck in a little room. With a basin under the bed. And a nurse to slide it under the sheet. With no possibility of choosing what you want to have on your plate. With no possibility of seeing women and everything that goes along with that. No the friend would rather leave before those things happened. In that case, T concludes, the friend will leave first. A pause is not necessarily a sign of embarrassment. One is not obliged to speak, it is distracting to look at the passers-by. The waitress asks them to settle the bill. T miraculously discovers some change in his pockets. Yes, the ex-friend continues as he unzips his wallet, T has as much chance as he does to survive. Fifty-fifty, there's no way to know in advance. The two men stare at each other again, which one is the most decrepit. Nonetheless, says the ex-friend, a clear winner the second time round, it would be good if T said what he wanted, in case he were buried first. Would he have any last wishes. Does he have a wish that he'd like granted, in addition of course to the text they swore to act. T has no opinion on the subject. Oh yes, he wonders if he's not going to ask to be thrown into the dustbin along with the garbage. A T in a garbage bag, among the vegetable peelings. Really funny, right. T always had a good sense of humour, says the ex-friend to get him out of his dustbin. And so, where will T be buried. Oh, T would rather go off in smoke. Reach the sky, the clouds. Hey, becoming seed for the blackbirds. Do blackbirds eat bones or ashes. The ex-friend cannot say and the waitress struggles to give him an answer. Does that girl even speak our language. T asked his question loud and clear, though. The ex-friend comes up with an explanation and the girl leans over the tables again with her rag. OK. If T were to be incinerated, the friend would go to the columbarium. It wouldn't be too convenient but he'd act in front of his niche. Many people would be invited, says the ex-friend, thinking of those little boxes. And if T should finally be buried, the friend would go to his cross and play his part, even if T were to be buried at the other end of the earth. The ex-friend waits for thank-yous, which do not seem to be forthcoming.

And what about T. Does he know where he has to go. Does he know where he has to go when the friend passes away, when this man sitting in front of T has done his time on earth and newspapers have written that one artist is no longer of this world. For T doesn't have to worry, the friend assures him, the newspapers are sure to report his demise, T can't miss it, it'll be printed in black and white. Certainly not on the first page. Certainly not in big letters but in small print, for we know how much artists count in this world: artists count for peanuts. On this topic, T can go him one better. The space they give to theatre is microscopic. He should have thought twice and become a football player instead of choosing the stage. He would have the thighs of a bison and whole crowds would know his face. But why on earth didn't T stay in films, the ex-friend asks, venturing into swampy territory. He had his place waiting for him, leaving was a mistake, repeats the lesson-giver, already sunk in the mud half way up his body. T becomes interested in birds.

211

That sparrow there, the one begging round the cups, what a bold one. And also interested in the waitress' butt, when she leans over the tables, but there's no reason to say that out loud, that's included in T's contract on earth.

OK, says the ex-friend who wants to get it over with as quickly as possible. T should keep in mind this one thing. The friend comes from that village in the country. T must have memories of it, he came there on holiday the year they both turned nineteen. He couldn't have forgotten the dog. Don't you remember, the dog who got away and decimated the farmer's rabbits. T couldn't have forgotten their evenings in front of the record player. The cigarettes. The night rides on the mopeds and how they tumbled over onto the railroad embankment. He couldn't have forgotten Marie-Paule. And the barn, no, it's impossible T could have forgotten that. The friend and T fought so much about that barn and about cigarettes in that barn. About the hay that catches fire and about some people lying in that hay. It took ten years for the friend to reimburse the wooden frame. Ten years and his father hadn't been very accommodating. Not to mention the price of the machinery and hay. But T. T doesn't even remember his own address. As for his childhood, he thinks it never happened. Burning hay, that doesn't ring a bell, he never tumbled over and he has no interest in dogs. Not to mention rabbits. And as for girls in barns, there is a lot of sorting out to be done and it would take him a whole day. But all right, let's try. What was she like. Tall or pudgy. Was she one with a moped.

OK, OK, says the ex-friend who wants to get it over with still more quickly. Anyway, here's the name of the village. He writes a name on the bill and puts it into T's fingers. T has to take the bus, unless he takes his car, but T doesn't have a vehicle, just two feet and two legs. Or better still, T can take the train and get off at such and such station and from there call a taxi to get to the cemetery. It's not far but when the time comes, it's very possible that T will no longer have the use of his legs, the ex-friend says to himself, since deterioration has clearly set in. Above all, he must not forget the script. That the ex-friend hopes, as their play has it, to rise from the grave immediately is not pronounced by his mouth, but T gets the message perfectly.

ᵃ THAT'S NORMAL FOR AN INSENSITIVE MAN like you, the ex-friend had said at the pavement cafe, a sentence T hadn't noticed then. It comes back to him during the nights, when at the hour before the dawn he wakes up and looks at the sky edged by curtains. Not sensitive. T wouldn't have thought so. He would have thought he wore his heart taped to his sleeve. He studies the sentence. It doesn't seem to have been said out of envy. It doesn't seem to have been said with bitterness, the friend pronounced these words at the end of a fine conversation. Those words came out and they were neither a criticism nor an attack. Just a casual statement. Not sensitive. But what is he, then. What does he have, if not sensitivity. If T didn't have the sensitivity to carry him through life and, more important, on stages, where, after all, he had shone for years for God's sake, you can even see it in magazine articles, T didn't make it up. What do you mean, not sensitive. T had tons of feelings. He suffered more than a horse. He felt love, for example, that impersonal emotion one recognizes in others. Of course he has devoured his own fair share of it and if there's one thing T watches attentively, it is loving couples. On their faces he can recognize things he tasted, oh Lord, a very long time ago. Love, that business is the same for everyone. They make mountains out of it but it's impossible to add one ounce of originality to it. And ditto for all feelings. Anger is red, it roars. Jealousy badmouths people and twists its mouth. But all that is so well known.

So that's why, when all is said and done—concludes T at the evening of his career with a hundred shows on his head, the beginnings of a pain in his knee and acid coming up from his oesophagus after meals—he was able to inhabit those roles and rock whole audiences. T: an indeterminate man, who changes costumes at will like a paper doll. A man who has admirably mastered the whole gamut of emotions. You ring T and at will he can show you: hope, sadness, doubt, gaiety. He has never descended into the core of his being, he has merely observed. He has reproduced things, he's been a copier. But now his career is over.

RAINY DAYS ARE LONG AND IN THE HOTEL you're driven out by the chambermaids. They are old and nothing can faze them. Old ladies. T knows that age

group well. He knows it because he breathed it in
deeply at the beginning of his reign, when he would
go into the foyer of the theatre to be reassured that
he had acted well. The old ladies were always present. Old women are what remains when everything
else has gone to hell. If a war smashed the world to
pieces, at the very end you'd still see an old lady in
the ruins, poking up the ashes. A sparse gathering
has its quota of old women. Not that he adores them
but T, by the force of circumstance, has spent a lot
of time with them. He knows how to handle them.
He knows what they are made of: thirty-six per cent
of sourness and thorns and thirty-six per cent of
bottled up freshness. He knows that perceptiveness
and chatter fill up the remaining per cent, whatever
that may be, T doesn't bother himself with mental
arithmetic any more. He even played an old lady,
come to think of it. Ah, what laughter there was.
They had put a wig on him. An apron and inside it,
T's body, which, thank God, has nothing feminine
about it, was like a tree-trunk trimmed with an axe.
A blue chequered apron that emphasized his vigorous nature. Yes, under this costume, T seemed even
more masculine than he was. All you could see were
the hairs under the skirt and the stubble round his

lipstick. The bra was a stiff prosthesis in the middle of his thorax. T thanks life for not having given him boobs and not having to harness himself like a workhorse. He also thanks it for being able to open his knees and not having to act as if he were hiding the treasure of Tutankhamen between his legs. When he was the old lady, the efforts T had to make to hide it were exhausting, he kept showing his underpants and his female acting partners kept him on tenterhooks all the time. T, we saw your underpants. They're white today, T. Don't show your underwear. T, I saw your crotch. Sitting down and getting up without showing anything is indeed one of the things T never perfectly mastered on stage. His entrance got a laugh. He would be all bent over to represent old age and had a rasping voice. They had given him a barrel to carry, a red one if T remembers correctly, and in his clogs walked with his feet turned in. What was the name of that dumb country girl again. Louison, Marion, Rigaudon or some such invention. When he appeared, the audience would be stunned and recoil. Then explode, when from the fat old mouth fell the fake little voice.

If it's raining hard, T waits down in the lobby while the women finish making up his room. When the lift is called and he hears them getting on with the laundry trolley, he takes the stairs back up. It would be unpleasant to run into them. They would lecture him. They'd say you have to get some air, instead of hanging around in your room. Instead of lying on your bed every blessed day. They'd say it's bad for your mood and your health. T should get out and go for a walk. T's going to get depressed if he doesn't clear his mind. A strange shortcut, T says to himself: a mind grafted onto legs. A very tight string binds minds and legs, according to women. They always say you have to get some air. From the first to the last, they think it's good to walk, to go from one place to another, even if you have nothing to do there. Where did they get that from, where does science say that one must walk. Walking. But T does not walk. He sits down wherever he can and he thinks his legs don't have to tire themselves out. Getting tired would be dangerous. Old age goes together with getting tired. No one has ever seen an old man who wasn't tired and if you spare yourself you might be able to avoid fatigue. T is not old and he doesn't seem old, because he feels energetic. Hair, belly, are of no importance. What counts is energy and, on this point, T has resources. He's vigorous as a young bull. Except of course when he climbs a flight of stairs. It is good to take little breaks on the way up, to allow the thought process to develop without jolts. Only Léona, he discovers as he puts his foot on the first step, never talked about walking.

She's certainly the only woman on earth. Léona didn't talk about legs, exercise and muscle tone. She would disappear at certain times into places which were for T black holes. At a certain time, she would shut herself up in her office and T, through the keyhole, could see nothing. And he didn't hear much either. Yes, there was that huge ball and that hoop in her office. There was the stationary bike and the rowing machine and pieces of machinery that made the office look, without pushing it, like a fitness centre, but Léona had said she didn't use them. She never used those machines. Those things belonged to a friend and when she came to get them, Léona could get her office back. T had no problem believing it, because not one drop of perspiration had ever flowed down Léona's skin and because Léona's muscles had never shown signs of flabbiness. That pure woman. His wife. The only one who'd given him a springboard, but T, after his somersault, fell on the wrong side of it and never played in a film again. He said no to the cinema. He decreed that he was worthless and it's better to save oneself for theatre audiences. The audience of old ladies and children who come with their classes as an alternative to punishment. The Chinese would never see T. The Americans would never know how incompetent that fat T is. They would sleep soundly without ever having heard of him and, as a result, their life would be, without their even guessing it, greatly improved. Never but never would T play the fool in front of a camera again. He would never allow himself to be ridiculed again. No longer will he turn his head a hundred and thirty times saying ah for a link shot in front of a camera. T, even if he isn't very clever, understood that his talent is not transplantable. His talent is not pure. His talent cannot be ripped away from the stage, or T would feel without clothes, without a skeleton, and would vanish into nothingness. T's talent is made of a box with three walls and a plank floor. Of a thick curtain, in which it is nonetheless amusing to make holes and peek out at the other side. That talent consists in two stagehands, a lighting technician and at least one acting partner to play opposite him. T's talent sits down in a theatre and applauds. It runs to the bathroom at the end. T's talent. How to explain that to Léona. Léona never knew those things. On stage, T dissolves. His wives and children always had a hard time recognizing him. If T could have thought of acquiring a tougher surface, he probably would have resisted and his wives would have found something to get a grip on. Everything went the other way. At least I've experienced things, T consoles himself, thinking of his ten thousand evening performances. Next to them, the months of shooting in the desert are cat's piss. Above all, avoid thinking of the piece of rubbish he acted in.

He turns his key in the lock. He keeps wondering by the way what's the use of a key in here. A squad of women comes and goes at all hours in his room and in this hotel, he has the privacy of a baby. No, above all, forget that piece of rubbish. Thinking of it means twelve sleepless nights. Means pains and acid reflux. The producers, what idiots, how the hell did they come up with those execrable shots. There were others where T was good. When he was seen from far away and melted into the group. The others were not watchable. Twenty-eight close-ups where he was bad and fifteen medium shots in which he was absolutely awful. His voice sounded so phoney it made your two eardrums burst.

LET'S GO ON. T HAD BEEN UP TO NOW what is called a force of nature. He was built like a Turk and certain heads would lower imperceptibly before him. T had always done whatever suited him. He had always taken whatever he wanted. He'd never had to wait for anything. He never thought further than his belly or his nose. He was never visited by doubt. Yes or no—such had been T's answers up to now, nothing in between. T had not yet found himself in the position of saying yes while feeling that no was the right answer because a yes was right round the corner. T used to laugh at people who cry easily. T's lachrymal glands always regulated themselves on their own and T had never thought about their mechanism. He would have done better to think about it. He should have studied it when it was still functioning, because now there seems to be something like leaks and T finds himself inconveniently overwhelmed. The thing happens for no particular

222

reason. T is sitting in the park, nothing new about that. The change appears when animals from everywhere converge, yes, that's what happens, animals start converging and if T's problem now has become animals, it wouldn't surprise him. Dogs, to be precise, coming up to him with their tails wagging, as if T was hiding a rib steak in his pocket. There's nothing to eat in T's pocket, for God's sake, but nothing is more clingy than a dog who wants to sniff you up. There is nothing more ridiculous. Nothing more embarrassing than a dog pressing up against your crotch. But dogs have not yet learnt to decode insults. Nothing weakens you more than innocent eyes and a tongue coming out to lick you and then, suddenly, that damn surge of emotion again.

Normally, that species kept a low profile. The dogs, without T doing anything, would give his bench a wide berth. Never a dog, let's say, five years ago, would have dared lick his hand that way. It wouldn't have felt free to sniff even his foot without his permission. T had a natural authority about him. And never would babies have dared climb up on his bench right after being lifted from their strollers and never would their mothers or nannies casually come sit next to him with their cookies and rattles to strike up a conversation. T can frown, remain mute, nurture his bad mood, be impolite all he wants—dogs, babies and babysitters don't give a hoot. Toddlers climb up on his bench and hold out their sweet little faces and T goes into a swoon. It seems to him there's been a mistake in casting when those ladies entrust him with their children while they go to the store or God knows where, in his terror T goes deaf. The little guys thrash about and begin to yell. T is subjected to the fond looks from all the females walking by anywhere near.

OK, ENOUGH OF THAT. Back to the real world. In the real world, there is Efina, who is waiting and not waiting for T. Efina who goes about her business, like any self-respecting woman who has to occupy her mind. Efina who walks her dog, and sometimes her dog's friend, so he should not be melancholy. When cleaning up the house, from time to time, she finds a hair between the cushions. A short, white hair that looks like the mane of a certain animal soon to become extinct. Yes, but Puck too has white hairs, if you look carefully, right under his throat.

It would be surprising if T's hairs could still be found on the couch. Life had drawn them together but then each of them was thrown back to their own side. T to the side of hippopotamuses in grassy ditches, puffing muzzles, nostrils full of flies and fat bodies not exactly made of lace. Efina to the asphalt side, with streets that are swept and rinsed down once a week, to skies where birds fly, houses where someone thinks with eyes lost in space and you can see dust collecting into balls under the furniture.

Cleaning out her attic, she finds a pile of magazines devoted to the art of the theatre. She leafs through them before throwing them out. This one for example, a panorama of actors who count on the stages of this country. The issue is not very old, it's from a few years back. Would T's name be in it. Yes, there it is. Here at the back. Under the heading: The Old Guard.

Efina has not seen T again and besides, she stopped thinking of him, or if she did think of him, she pushed him away with exasperation. What is that man doing, coming back into her mind like that. There is no room for him in there. Naturally, if T showed up again with a flower at his lapel, clean

225

and smoothly shaven, with a bouquet of red roses and a declaration of love on his lips. If T appeared smiling coyly and swearing he couldn't forget her and had become young and fit in the meantime. Yes, Efina might perhaps give him a foot in the door. If someone rang her bell and who would be there, it would be T and, seeing him there, Efina's heart would be three hundred per cent sure. If her heart could be lucid and aim right instead of making mistakes. But Efina's heart is a strange machine that races for all kinds of people. It suffers from blindness and lack of savvy, which is regrettable, for a heart. A heart should see through things and be well advised, and instead, what happens. Efina sees flames when someone is only striking a match. The match burns up and Efina finds herself with charcoal. Efina's heart is great when it comes to giving her a line. It turns beggars into princes. Friends into lovers. Outlaws into respectable people and vagabonds into men. It confuses certain feelings and has the unfortunate tendency to lose the distinction between love and pity. Is Efina's heart even capable of love, you may ask. It would be wise to look for a secure retreat beforehand, though.

Efina

She's never happy but it's not her fault. Nothing can satisfy her. Not her friends. Not her work. Not her dog. The dog has grown old. Efina didn't think dogs could become elderly. All the dogs before Puck disappeared prematurely, due to accident or illness. But Puck is really tough and it seems he's making his way towards old age. He walks up the stairs slowly. In the park, he won't play. He just lies there under a bench. He can't manage to scratch himself on the back and when he has an itchy spot, it's Efina's hand that has to go into action. His slow-ness is worrying. He makes prolonged stops during which he seems to be lost in thought. He is scolded by Efina, who is still well preserved and has pins and needles in her legs. Don't get lost in space like that. He no longer lifts up his head to look at her. Only his eyes move and they have become wider and more eloquent. From close up. But had Efina already noticed them. You can see wrinkles piled up under his nice brown eyes, so that now Puck has the gaze of a monkey. Given the situation, if Puck retired or wished to leave, it would be all right with Efina and she can see the moment coming when she would go down to the park alone. She can see the moment coming when entering her flat will no longer be a celebration but a desert echoing with her calls while her hand came to rest on a carotid artery.

Efina's friends, who see all that from the outside and thus have some distance, feel free to give her advice. They speak of certain injections and what a dog's life is. A dog's life, what else is it but running in the sun. Running in the rain. Running with a muzzle grazing the ground and discovering smells. Living totally in his body because the head is not required. A dog's life, what is it when health is failing. When one is handicapped, or worse, paralysed. Can you still be a dog when you walk at a mile an hour. Can you still be a dog when you suffer from rheumatism and your heart is no longer a gleaming piston. Finally, can you still be a dog when you no can longer chew your food and little females no longer drive you wild. The friends know the answer and they say it for Efina. No, one can no longer be a dog. Past a certain limit, you can speak of decline and taking walks with decline on a leash is horrible. Does Efina want to inflict this spectacle on herself, does she also want to inflict it on all the other dog-walkers. If so, let her keep going. Does she want to respect the animal and prove her affection for him.

If so, there is just one thing to do and a competent person will come say goodnight to her dog and the dog will be grateful to her. Efina cannot decide. Puck is certainly a burden. She doesn't need the leash any more, she carries him on the stairs. The dog takes advantage of this to lick her and they both get something out of that. The friends give her a number. The number is on the table and Efina's eyes are constantly settling on it.

Puck had arrived at Efina's with T. If T returned, he would see Puck again and he would be shocked to find him slow and wrinkled in his basket. He could not fail to be struck by the dog's transformation. He might then count up all the years he missed. All those weeks and months when he wasn't home, during which, little by little, the dog lost his youth. He would make an act of contrition and apologize. Or T would be sitting on a bench and Puck in front of him by chance would start to die. T, lost in his thoughts, would suddenly recognize the dog and he would take him in his arms. Efina would run up and Puck, between the two of them, would breathe his last. But God knows where T is prowling now. All right, let's be honest, from time

to time, Efina does think of T. But only fleetingly.
Yes, the idea may come to her that their time
together wasn't such a disaster after all and it would
perhaps be good to have it back. Something did
exist and, when you look at it closely, that thing
wasn't so shaky, it was solid and if it broke, that
doesn't mean it was worthless, it just means they
didn't fix it. At other times, thinking of T, she'd like
to go back in time to erase him completely and she
thinks herself blessed to have seen T vanish down
the hall for good. Even if, to be perfectly sincere,
the last time she saw him, T was not in a hallway
and was not about to run away because of a domestic quarrel. He was standing on a stage. Yes, Efina
did go there, even though she wrote to him to the
contrary. She did go to that theatre, she did go see
T perform and strut round with those girls. She
bought a ticket. She went neither to the first nor the
last performance but to an ordinary show. She sat
down in the third row and the lights went down.
On either side of Efina, old ladies unwrapped
sweets. The curtain rose. T entered and a wave
went through the audience. He acted and, as far as
that goes, there was no cause for complaint. His acting is perfect. He reached summits from which he

cannot descend. Acting is in T's flesh. No. Even if
the play was outdated and not that exciting, Efina
appreciated it, thanks to T's acting. Thanks to the
actresses, who did their job well. Efina applauded
and her hands, along with the others', called T back
to take his bow. But one thing was troubling. A line
appeared on the stage, when T was revealed in all
his glory. A sharp, cutting line impossible to separate from T. That line was, how to put it. In his acting, T was extremely brilliant. On stage he was
swearing his love and Efina witnessed something
she had already seen somewhere. It's odd, T shows
everywhere that he's a great virtuoso and never
leaves his virtuosity behind. He takes it with him
through life. He takes it along to whichever woman
he's living with and clever indeed would be the one
who could say what T feels deep down and for
whom squeezes and swells the tendon that serves
him for a heart. From the third row, Efina saw T
swoon from very close up. The resemblance was
stupefying and she almost could have thrown herself into his arms. She saw him love for real. She
saw him go through terrible pain and her body
trembled for that poor T. All that got applause and
T can do it again every night. It's odd, Efina could

not rid herself of that precise thought. At the beginning of the bows, she stood up. In the midst of the applause, she disturbed everyone, walked over a row of feet and, as T was bowing up there, she escaped from the theatre.

And there again, and once and for all, Efina thought T was not for her. He grew even smaller and she never saw him again. She never saw him again. Let's see. Has she seen him another time. Well, it's possible. It is possible that that time in the theatre was not quite the very last. The next to last perhaps, because Efina may have seen T afterwards prowling under her windows. She thought of waving to him but her hands remained on the windowpane. She drew back her head and observed her ex-darling without his realizing it. He was standing on the pavement. He looked as if he didn't know what he wanted. Sometimes he stared at the windows or walked towards the building. Sometimes he wanted to talk to people who avoided him and walked away quickly. You would have thought he was begging, if he hadn't been standing there with his nose in the air looking at her windows, at the wrong floor of course, as if to say: Here lived the great T. From here, the great T escaped and has not yet recovered from the affront he received when no one came to look for him. Here resides a little lady and may her name be forgotten. Here T will never again set foot. So why are you hanging around under my windows, muttered Efina, with a good view of his bald spot.

T left for Mars and Efina never saw him again. Never again seen and never even thought of again. Scraping noises and loud breathing, heavy footsteps and thumps may well have resounded at intervals from the other side of the door. But as that door remained carefully locked, that man was never spotted again. Never thought of. Forgotten. Erased. Dead and buried. And then one can go peacefully about one's business. But of course, obviously. One must expect people of that sort to come back and bother you. If the whole story were to be told. If everything had to be laid on the table, you might say. You might say the time with T below her windows was not absolutely strictly speaking the last. You might mention a final last time but it didn't really count at all. Is it worth dwelling on.

That time was in the park, where else, and T was on a bench and not in the sandbox. T was on a bench and Efina was walking by him. Nothing is simpler. A man is sitting on a bench and a woman walks by. The woman does not have an animal with her, how strange, it's because he's disabled but that cannot be seen on her. The woman who walks by the man gave him kisses once, long ago, and told him over and over, long ago, that she would love him till the end of the earth. And the man sitting on that bench was mad about that lady to the point of swearing that he would never again touch other ladies. The two perjurers are facing each other and they cannot escape. Just my lousy luck, stammers the man to be funny. And as for the woman, she does not speak. The woman has been petrified and what she thinks has also turned into little stones. Two statues staring at each other in the park. After what could have been several decades, the woman makes a terrible effort to thaw out a little word. A little word is thawed out and she asks if she can sit on the bench. She doesn't feel like sitting but, at this point, you say whatever wants to come out and T puts a hand on the bench, which means: Come, sit. Efina sits on the bench and they no longer have to

look at each other. A few seasons later, one of them
turns his head slightly and the other does the same.
The eyes try to see each other but it's a bit prema-
ture and they take the path to the lawn again. No
need to hurry when one is convalescing. Slow and
steady. Things happen little by little and all things
come to him who waits. Or to her. Efina feels a bit
more mobile and she clears her throat in preparation.
That seems to wake up her neighbour too, who
applies himself to a few preparatory throat-clearings,
and the rehearsal can begin. But who will speak first.
No one knows the script, or is the scene a pan-
tomime. T's timid eyes graze over Efina's knees.
Efina sighs. Nothing else is possible. T tries another
throat-clearing and sighs too. It looks like he's going
to say something. But no, the great actor is silent,
probably because everything has its price and no
ticket has been bought. T's hand on the bench. The
bench was green but it is turning brown. T's hand
fiddles around peeling off scales of paint. That hand
of T's is not far from the little hand of his lady, he
can't miss it. A fat, red hand on the peeling wood.
A hand making a small noise as it rips off the paint.
It could land on top of the other one. It could touch
the little hand and everything could begin again.

Both hands feel the urge and the temptation and the bench's centre of gravity weighs the hands down with all its force. But one should not think of all these vain attempts. Not think of all the times the hand was grabbed. All the times the thing was pursued, only to escape every time. Not think of the preliminaries or take great care not to give up and go on another ride. That's the way it is and it's unfortunate. Something does not want to die but no one can take hold of that thing. Both have reached this conclusion at the same time. They relax and Efina steals a glance at her neighbour. He is worn out and lacks charm. T steals a glance at this lady: she's bizarre and crazy-looking. She's wearing shoes with thick white soles and the tip reinforced with leather. Shoelaces thick as doubled ʒ's.

THE DOG HAS BEEN REPLACED. Yes, Puck is dead, like all the dogs that entered this house. Efina's heart went soft, she cried when Puck fell asleep in the vet's hands. The new dog is not very likeable. It's the first time this has happened but Efina must admit, this dog is not likeable. He looks at you spitefully. Efina chose him for the colour of his coat. A butter-caramel coat. She forgot to look at his face and back at the house she thought the dog was sulking. She was affectionate with him, she took him for walks, she bought expensive cans. But the dog stares continuously at everyone with a nasty look. He has a grudge against people. People get out of the way and fewer walkers say hello to Efina in the park. The dog wanted to bite a child and the explanations nearly ended in a fight. Aside from that, Efina and her dog have found suitable arrangements for their life together. It has been established that the dog will not need to sleep on the couch while she watches TV. In exchange, Efina has the right to rest her feet on his back to warm them. He agrees to wear a muzzle but Efina allows him to yap at home. He has the right to growl at strangers while Efina calms them down but he must be welcoming to boyfriends. Boyfriends do not remain for long but it's important for a dog to get used to coming across different bodies between his bowl and his mat. A pink body, a brown body, a thick body, a strong body, a brown body and so on.

Efina in her neighbourhood recognizes an actor. He's nice-looking, slim, he's her age and lives near her building. You see his name on posters.

They say hello when they come across each other. Efina admires him and, little by little, she begins to think of him apart from the theatre. She runs into him often in the neighbourhood. They have little chats on the street or after shows, in the foyer. The actor asks her to go for a drink and a great love unfurls its wings in one night. They have a relationship for two or three years, then that love loses a wing and Efina, from one day to the next, doesn't see him any more. She meets another actor. Because he's modest, this one is not well known, although he is talented, and that's what Efina likes about him. She keeps her nugget of gold well hidden. If the actor suddenly died, she would be the only one to have discovered him, she thinks, as she strokes the forehead of the dark-haired actor on the pillow. Who grows tired of her and goes off with a dark-haired woman. But Efina before her door finds her first actor once again. He's standing there with his hands in his pockets. He apologizes, he realizes that she must be the woman of his life. He also needs a roof over his head and a place to stay and Efina shelters him again for a while. The old ashes are stirred and they blow hard on them. You don't get bored with this man. Love is included in the fun. Japanese lanterns light up Efina's windows once more. Then love moves on to another woman. Efina gets married. Her husband is not an actor at all. They separate. She moves. Any change is good for you. She moves into a flat she can't afford. There is a room that remains empty. Dust piles up in it, it is distressing to open it up and look at those four walls. No matter how tightly it's locked, you can feel its space through the wall and walking past its door gives you the creeps. The dog does not want to sleep there. There would have been room, though, and Efina could have put his mat in there for him.

Efina goes to the theatre assiduously. It has become difficult to find men. And when you find one you live in fear he might leave. And they do leave, because they don't want to live in fear. They leave for fresh, pink women but that's not the reason. They leave because love has stopped beating. Other women are absolutely not the reason. Physique is not important. Age doesn't count, that's what Rashid, her new boyfriend, assures her. They're sitting at a pavement cafe and Rashid is holding her hand. With the other hand he lifts a tall, slim glass and drinks the cocktail with a straw. Efina and Rashid are drinking with two straws from the same glass. Couples come and go on the pier. Rashid hopes to live with Efina for the rest of his life. He's sick of break-ups and going from bed to bed. He found Efina and he hopes that love will hold out to the end. He is tall, reassuring. He has a paunch but, compared with men his age, it is a very small paunch. His paunch shrinks quite visibly when you compare it with many men of his generation and Rashid would even be attractive if you put him side by side with certain specimens. He is talking in front of the waves. It's their first holiday, an unexpected weekend by the sea. There are few tourists. At the start of the season, the sun is never very strong. Rashid absentmindedly sucks up the alcohol with Efina's straw. He says that a woman is a friend. Not a girlfriend, a friend. He wants them to be together as equal to equal. Mind and character are of prime importance. Rashid's eyes are from time to time carried away by a bust or legs walking along the pier but they come back in a minute and his hand holds Efina's more tightly.

A MAN WHO HAS HIS EYES CLOSED, you don't want to disturb him. With a man lying on the floor, you'd call the hospital, but a man sitting with his eyes closed in a cafe does not arouse suspicion. People point to him laughingly. The waitresses slip him a cushion. They think he has a stiff neck. They take advantage of the situation to exchange all sorts of jokes. You can double the take if you're lucky enough to have in your cafe a man sitting with his eyes closed. The customers stay longer just for the laughs. They order a third round. They play childish pranks like putting a paper over his mouth and watching it flutter. Putting a plastic decoration on his head. Bending his hand until it seems to give you the finger. Arranging his hands over his belly as if he were praying. The sighs that escape from that chest increase the customers' merriment. It's not every day you have a life-size doll. His cheeks empty and swell. Each time the doll moans, the customers answer him. Heeeeee, goes the sleeping man. Shut up, cries a drunk. Heeeeee, goes the sleeping man. You want a glass of beer, says another, pouring him liquid. Pfffffffff, goes the man with his eyes closed, and the liquid runs down his trench coat buttoned up to the top, even though it's visibly too tight for him. The poor man, he's not comfortable, says a waitress who hides a mother's heart beneath her apron. She leans over the snorer to unbutton his coat. The people sitting at the tables crane their necks. They lift themselves up to see better. Under the trench coat there is nothing. Nothing but fleece and skin.

This guy's an odd one, says the waitress, modestly adjusting the coat over her Sleeping Beauty. She's seen her share in this bar. She's learnt in the course of a career spent striding over tiled floors that customers are unhappy people. They come to bars to fill their needs. She squeezes the thick shoulder affectionately. A few off-colour anatomical comments burst forth but the merriment is gone. There's something abnormal about this sleeper but appearances can be deceiving. The customers leave one by one. There's just T on his seat now. The two waitresses, with their miniskirts and legs that would be better off covered, take advantage of the lull to rearrange the plastic roses on the tables. Wash the dishes. Do the cash register. Smoke a cigarette. It's morning. A second batch of customers. These new people don't know what's going on and when they make comments about the man who's snoring away, puffing and moaning, the waitresses inform them. This customer came in very early. He ordered herb tea. The tea remained in front of him and after one or two hours the waitresses put their fingers on the cup. They dipped their index finger in the cold water, made the decision to take it away and emptied it out behind the bar. The saucer was put away and the bag returned to the box of camomile. The bill disappeared in the same way and the waitresses agreed among themselves to pay it with their tips. They'd never seen this customer before. They've had ample time to examine his face and, even if you have to bend your knees a little to do that, they're positive, this customer never came in here before. They are absolutely sure of it, they would remember. It's not every day you see a customer with a face like that. A face like a monument. Something like the head of a lynx. No, a Sphinx, the one you see in Egypt.

The waitresses take him under their wing. They come real close to him, and pressing his shoulder cautiously, whisper encouragements to bring him back to earth. But nothing works and the second batch of customers is beginning to find him pretty funny. One customer suggests laying him out on the wall seat so he can be comfortable. Another says this guy must be on sleeping pills. The waitresses agree. He must have come in around eight this morning. It'll soon be past three and the sitting man doesn't budge. They're worried, because they're going home and they would have liked to know what he'll say when he wakes up. They take off their aprons and tell the colleagues who are taking over now what to do. Above all do not disturb him. The guy is very tired. Be sure to tell him that Christine and Mireille are the ones who paid for his tea. Yeah yeah yeah, we'll tell him. And now they begin their day.

The cafe is full and the waiters don't have the time to take care of this guy. Still, they do have to straighten him up when he slumps over to the side. You don't want him falling on the tile floor. It takes two for this, because the man is rather corpulent; it's entertaining to watch the old waiter and the waitress on each side of him trying to straighten him up. The waiter takes him under the armpit. The waitress takes him from the other side, they count one, two and they sit him up straight. His legs aren't too solid any more, they roll every which way and the man would be inclined to slide forward under the table.

Let's push the table so it props up his belly. The head also rolls forward, too. What's going on here, mumbles the waitress as she takes away the cushion they'd rolled at the back of his neck. The head nods forward. Careful, says the waiter, and both of them have to put their hands on his forehead so it doesn't bang on the table and make the customers shout, and above all so there shouldn't be any blood. He's really smashed, says the waiter who's used to drunks. The hands of the waiter and waitress are joined on T's forehead. Their hands depose the big head gently on the table, not too gently though because they don't have much time. The waitress takes T's arm and slides it underneath his cheek, toppling the head. The waiter does the same from the other side. They make sure the legs are straight so there won't be problems and they can't be blamed if the customer hurt himself or anything. Anyway, there are witnesses. The witnesses think it sure doesn't look right, a man collapsed over his arms like that, he's sick or what.

The evening is quiet. When she goes near him, the waitress checks the face lying on its side over his arms. He doesn't look like he wants to wake up. His eyelids are not really closed and if you stand directly in front of him you can see part of the pupils. He's asleep or what, asks the waitress and the customers get up and look through the opening and give their opinion. He's asleep. He's pretending. He's not asleep. He's dead. The old waiter feels compelled to put his forefinger on the body and look for the carotid. He's alive. The waitress sticks out her pinky, too. The waitress can't feel a thing. Has his heart stopped beating. He's warm though. She raises one of his eyelids, a vacant discoloured white. He has blue eyes, says the waitress, and curious people come over and lift the eyelid. The waiters' eyes look more often at the clock, which is signalling closing time.

Enter some drunks who get called to order. The gentleman is sleeping. They can't manage to agree on what they should do with the gentleman. The waiter's for calling on the customers for help and depositing him on the pavement where he'll finish sleeping it off. The waitress is not sure he's drunk. He's been here since the morning. So what, says the waiter, who has seen his share of comas before. He's seen plenty of guys in that state, you would've left them for dead. The waitress thinks they have to call the police. She has the idea, but how come no one thought of it before, to put her hands in his pockets and take out his wallet. Nothing in the outside pockets. The waiter puts his hand in the breast pocket. He's embarrassed, because of the hairs directly under his hand. His hand retreats. The guy doesn't have any clothes on, the waiters will be committing rape. A reprehensible act. Like robbing a corpse. Robbing a defenceless man. He announces what he's doing aloud. I'm looking for his wallet, he explains to the drinkers practically slumped over their glasses too. I just want to know his name, he says to the customers, who no longer remember their own. There's something, he says, wrinkling up his nose. The waitress says she hopes they find a number, so his wife can be alerted. The poor woman must be frantic. The waitress noticed the wedding ring that has made a line in his flesh. The waiter pulls out a passport. It has seen better days. It has seen better days all right and it's in an old format. The document is opened. They find a name. The guy's name is T. The name goes round by word of mouth to the very end of the room and the eardrums of the winos the furthest removed from this world. T doesn't mean a thing to anyone. Some get up to examine the remains. T, they say as they

stare at the leonine head. The waiter holds it by the
mane to pivot it round a little. The waitress, who
hasn't given up on informing the grief-stricken
wife, found a paper in a pocket. A theatre programme, that doesn't mean anything to anyone
either and the paper goes back into its hiding place.
We're closing, says the waiter. The waitress gets rid
of a customer and tells him to get the hell out. And
what about this one, says the waiter, activating his
broom. The chairs are turned upside down on the
tables, except for T's. His breath is rasping noisily
against the wood. Let's call an ambulance, decides
the waitress as she takes out a steaming basket of
dishes. At that moment, T comes back to life. He
moves his lips and mumbles. His hands clench and
his fingers move. He's moving, remarks the waitress. He's drooling, says the waiter who has dropped
his broom. I'm choking, T says, but no one can hear
him. We have to call the ambulance. Neither of
them moves. They watch T choking. It takes time
to die. A groaning rattle. An interruption. Is it
going to start again. Looks like it won't. Yes, there's
another rattle. It's painful. The waitress leaves to
make a phone call and comes back with her dish
towel. A death rattle, a suspension. You think it's

going to stop but it starts again even more loudly. He's tough, says the waiter. He wants to hang on, says the waitress. A death rattle. A long interval. Yes, long. Long. Is it going to start up again. Sure it will. But it seems like it won't. An interminable interval. An interval that hardly deserves the name. An interval that's transformed into eternity and an entrance into the other world.

A MAN IS GOING TO THE CEMETERY. He has a briefcase under his arm and, in his palm, sheets of papers are rolled up. He's sitting in the bus; he reads the papers silently, but his lips are moving and he's rehearsing with his eyes on the landscape. It seems that he hasn't noticed that he's surrounded by passengers and the bus is packed.

The man walks through the gate of a cemetery. It has been freshly painted, the gateway to the dead is green. Walk through it the other way and it's the gateway to the living. Good idea T had, to leave this world in July. People die in winter, but T has gone out through a door. T's gone out when the lights are on and everyone can see him. The sun is at the height of its curve. The nests are full. The thickets are overflowing. The meadows are swarming. T has left the world at harvest time. He's holding the scythe. He is the wheat. He's going out in the limelight and in splendour. There is no other way to make a successful exit in the theatre.

This man knows the theatre. He lives in it. The theatre is the invisible home he carries with him on his back, even into the cemetery where he has come to perpetuate the art of acting. The grave is easy to find. The flowers are drying, there are mattresses of them. T had no idea that all these flowers would come to his funeral. The man steps into the bouquets. He's standing on the grave. The sun lights up a portion of crown at the top of his head. A hairy crown, the pride of its proprietor: this skull has remained hairy, despite centuries and centuries. The rest isn't badly preserved either. The man clearing his throat and declaiming has a tanned, rugged face. The trees are trembling in a light breeze. He recites and speaks in the direction of the thing buried down there. He does both questions and answers, hurriedly, like a priest who has to say his mass. Behind the crosses, a young woman listens and looks on as she empties a watering can.

250

Another woman, no longer young but not yet old, is standing not far from the grave. She didn't want to stop, but her steps led her from the bus to the green gate. She didn't want to come, but her head figured out that the undertakers, girlfriends, wives and children would have dispersed a long time ago. She had no need for anyone and then her eyes happened to read an article in the paper and her feet brought her in front of a mattress of flowers where a man is gesticulating. He looks like an actor she saw a long time ago on the stage. The tombstone has not yet been erected. The name can be read on a wooden cross. The woman draws near, out of curiosity. What she hears interests her and she lingers a bit longer. The man waves for her to come closer to him on the grave. Here he must pause. He explains. This play is endless. If the woman could give him his cues it would all be over quickly.

The woman is standing on the grave with the scroll of paper in her hands. She deciphers her text. And so you have left us, recites the man. I am close to you and to all that concerns you, reads the woman. The trees move in the breeze. The sun has left the top of the man's head. The text unwinds.

There is nothing original about the costumes. The actress especially is not dressed to her advantage. The actor cuts a fine figure and you can sense he knows his trade. Nonetheless, if you listen carefully, you will notice a slight tendency to affectation and a rather repetitive diction. The set is very natural. The staging practically nonexistent. The actress does what she can, but she's clearly not up to the part. It's hard to tell if she has talent. For that, she would have to let herself go. Besides, her voice is too weak. Her voice is covered by the birds. The cemetery is the home of the birds.